THE BEACH B&B

A SUNNY ISLE OF PALMS NOVEL (BOOK 3)

GRACE PALMER

JOIN MY MAILING LIST!

Click the link below to join my mailing list and receive updates, freebies, release announcements, and more!

JOIN HERE:

https://sendfox.com/lp/19y8p3

ALSO BY GRACE PALMER
A SUNNY ISLE OF PALMS NOVEL (BOOK 1)

Sunny Isle of Palms

The Beach Baby

The Beach Date

The Beach B&B

The Wayfarer Inn

The Vineyard Sisters

The Vineyard Mothers

The Vineyard Daughters

Sweet Island Inn

No Home Like Nantucket (Book 1)

No Beach Like Nantucket (Book 2)

No Wedding Like Nantucket (Book 3)

No Love Like Nantucket (Book 4)

No Secret Like Nantucket (Book 5)

No Forever Like Nantucket (Book 6)

Willow Beach Inn

Just South of Paradise (Book 1)

Just South of Perfect (Book 2)

Just South of Sunrise (Book 3)

Just South of Christmas (Book 4)

THE BEACH B&B

Elaine Robbins is running out of options.

Bills don't pay themselves, and with her husband John gone, she doesn't know how she's going to afford to stay on the island she loves.

Renting out her spare rooms to strangers is a scary proposition, but what choice does she have?

Besides—after three years of too much quiet in her empty home, maybe a fresh face will help cure her loneliness.

But when her first guest, a travel writer named Finn, arrives, she starts to wonder if maybe she made a mistake. He's handsome and charming and warm—and somehow, those things feel a little bit scary.

Starting a new chapter means turning your back on the old one, after all.

Is she ready for that?

1

MOUNT PLEASANT, SOUTH CAROLINA—FIRST CITIZENS BANK AND TRUST

Elaine Robbins sat in front of the twenty-something loan officer in charge of her account and did her best not to squirm.

It was a little hard to stay still, though, because the plastic, modern-looking chair she'd been offered was shaped like an egg. Elaine kept sliding into the center of it, her feet lifting off of the floor. She felt like a child called into the principal's office.

"Have you considered downsizing?" the young man asked. The silver name plate on the corner of his desk said his name was Ebenezer. Elaine couldn't decide if that was a joke or not.

"Of course I have," she said. "But I'm here to look into other options."

A woman alone, widowed, childless—he knew what people saw when they looked at her. She knew quite well what they thought.

Why is she still living in that big old house?

Poor old thing, must be lonely.

Ebenezer leaned back in his chair and frowned. "I'm afraid there aren't many other options. Refinancing won't work."

"But I have proof of my retirement benefits. And I have half of John's pension, too. So—"

"Your income isn't the only problem, Miss Robbins."

"*Mrs.* Robbins," she corrected.

He apologized with a quick, indifferent smile. "I'm sorry, Mrs. Robbins, but the issue is also your credit score and existing debts. As I'm sure you know, you are behind on your mortgage, and…"

The rest of the conversation was white noise. Elaine had heard it all before. Too many times, in fact. Three other banks had told her the same thing.

She sleepwalked through the remainder of her appointment with Mr. Scrooge, then thanked him robotically and went back to her home —*her* home.

She'd insist on calling it that for as long as she possibly could.

With a sigh, she clomped up the stairs to the office, lugged a tattered cardboard box out of the closet, and began filing her papers away.

The scrawl of John's handwriting on the box lid made her laugh and roll her eyes at the same time. *Important Documents,* it said.

"These didn't do me any good at the bank. How 'important' can they really be?" she muttered to herself.

But she dutifully organized them in the system John had created decades ago. The box was almost as old as their marriage. He'd spent an entire weekend creating tabs for each sector of their life and explaining to Elaine how to file everything.

"Insurance forms in here," she remembered him saying as he flipped through the folders. "Bank statements in here, car registration in—"

"In the 'Car Registration' tab, I know. I get it," she'd said.

John had raised a finger to stop her. "No, actually. Car registration goes in the 'Automobile' tab."

Elaine smiled now at the memory. Just a few years since he'd passed and the folders were already overflowing without his yearly clear-out of what he termed the "non-essentials." John would be appalled by her organizational skills, though not particularly surprised.

As she walked into the dining room, Elaine stopped in front of the photograph hanging on the wall. The two of them smiled out from the frame, posing in front of a windowpane blue backdrop.

Picture Elaine looked younger and thinner—a few less wrinkles, a lot less grays. But John looked just the way he always did in her mind. She didn't know if that was because he hadn't changed much in the years since they'd taken the picture, or because the photograph she looked at every day was overriding her actual memories. She tried not to think about it too much.

"Another strike on the refinance," she said to him. "The third one, if you're keeping count. That means I'm out for good, right? You were the baseball fan, not me."

Either way, she was done. No more calling different banks and hoping for different outcomes. It was time to figure out another solution.

Elaine padded into the kitchen and pulled her leftovers from the fridge. She and John used to split the Tres Burritos platter from La Cocina, but now it made two meals for her. Three, if she was being responsible.

She microwaved her plate and walked back to the dining room table. The wooden leaf was still in the center from the dinner party they'd had a few weeks before John died. His brother and sister-in-law had been there that day. Elaine hadn't seen them in... why, it must be over a year, at least. A long time.

"I should take the leaf out, but that was always your job," she said. "Every time I do it, the table gets stuck on the tracks, and I can't push it back together. You'd probably say, *'You don't know until you try.'* Or *'Practice makes perfect.'* But I'd rather have a table that's too big than one split in half down the middle."

Elaine had considered asking Charlene's boyfriend, Noah, to come help her. But then she'd have to admit that the leaf had been in the table for three years. Would they imagine her sitting alone at the extra-long table night after night, surrounded by nothing but dust and no one but empty chairs?

"Maybe I'll sell it," she mused. "Put the money towards the mortgage. It wouldn't be much, but…"

Elaine wasn't crazy. She knew John was dead and gone. But sometimes, when she was talking out loud, she'd swear she could hear his response. It was like hearing someone talk from another room. After he died, someone told her she'd forget the sound of his voice one day, so she tried her darndest to cling to it.

"Your dad made this table as a wedding gift. I shouldn't sell it." She sighed. "But if I don't do something soon, I won't even have a dining room to put a table in. Maybe I should commit to the boarding house idea, but I don't know. Do I really want strangers in our house?"

The idea to rent out the empty rooms had come to her a few weeks earlier, but Elaine hadn't committed. As much as she wanted to hear someone else's voice aside from her own echoing off the walls, she didn't know if she was ready for such a big change.

"Guests would think I was crazy if they heard me talking to a photograph." She chuckled bitterly. "You probably think I'm crazy, too. And what do I know? Maybe I am. Crazy people rarely know they're crazy."

If John were here, he'd no doubt make some remark like, *Of course you're crazy. But that's why I love you.*

"This was supposed to be our dream house. You leaving me behind was never part of the dream." Elaine's lower lip wobbled. "A lot of things didn't go to plan, though."

They'd planned to have children. Three, maybe four. It was why they'd saved up for the big house by the beach. Each kid was going to have their own room and they were going to have picnics on the beach and teach them how to swim in the shallow surf.

Now, the rooms sat bare, empty, and expensive.

She fell quiet and finished her dinner. Some nights, the only thing worse than the silence was hearing her own voice go unanswered. John had always been a chatty one. *Jabbering John,* she called him whenever he really got going on one of his yarns. He was never one of the silent, stoic men she saw on television. He talked to Elaine—really, to anyone who was listening, but most especially Elaine—about anything and everything.

Everyone always tells you to marry your best friend. She'd done just that. But no one ever warned her that losing him would mean losing both friend and husband at the same time.

There wasn't much cleaning up to do: a single plate, a fork, and a Styrofoam carryout container. Sometimes, Elaine missed having a big load of dishes to wash up. Having someone to look after, to clean up for.

She slid her plate into the dishwasher and grabbed the takeout container. If she put it in the inside trash, it would start to smell. So, out to the big bin it would go.

Elaine slipped on her sandals and grabbed the back door handle. But before she could pull it open, she heard a faint whine.

She froze and tipped her head towards the vent hood over the stove. Once, a bird had built a nest on top of the vent opening, and the entire nest—baby birds included—had fallen down the shaft and gotten stuck inside. Elaine had frantically sent John up on the roof to reel them out with fishing line.

But the sound wasn't coming from the stove. It was coming from outside.

Elaine opened the door and stuck her head out, but she didn't see anything. Just palm trees swaying in the evening breeze. She listened for the sound she'd heard a moment ago.

Nothing, nothing…

And then, there, she heard it again. Faint but definite.

"Hello?" she called out softly. "Hello?"

She stepped out on the back porch, looked down her steps… and came face-to-face with a cat.

The animal was black with white mittens and a smattering of white across its face and ears. It sat at the foot of her stairs, paws politely crossed in front of him or her as though waiting to be invited up. When it saw her looking, it mewled and pawed at the ground.

"What is it?" Elaine asked. "What's the matter?"

The cat lowered its head and mewled again, a little louder and a little longer this time.

"Why are you making a pathetic sound like that? You look fine," she scolded. "What do you want?"

The cat tilted its head to the side as if weighing something. Then, decision reached, it bounded up the stairs in two easy pounces and sat down right in front of her feet, never taking its eyes off her.

She could almost see the thoughts passing behind its green eyes: *I'm here and I'm not leaving.*

"Oh no," Elaine said. "*I* can barely live here. Not for much longer, at least. You certainly cannot."

It tilted its head again quizzically and meowed.

"Do that all you want, but you can't stay here." Elaine closed her kitchen door behind her so the cat wouldn't bolt inside. "This is a cat-free house."

Another meow. This one a little more plaintive than the ones before. *You're not really saying no, are you?*

"No way," Elaine said firmly. "My husband is allergic to cats."

The words were out of her mouth before she even realized what she was saying. She'd always kept her distance from cats because of John's allergies. If she was around a cat for any period of time and then came home without washing her hands and changing her clothes, John could tell. His eyes would water and he'd start to sneeze.

"My husband *was* allergic to cats," she corrected. "But that doesn't change anything. You still can't come inside."

Kicking it up a notch, the cat sauntered forward and curled itself around Elaine's legs. It looked up at her and batted its green eyes. It was a begging face if Elaine had ever seen one.

"Nice try. Still no dice."

She walked around the cat to get to the dumpster and the cat let out a hoarse cry like she'd kicked it.

Elaine whirled back around and narrowed her eyes at the animal. "Drama queen! Was that really necessary?"

To punctuate the point, the cat cried out again.

Elaine sighed. "You can't stay here, dear."

She took a few steps towards the door. The cat snaked through her legs and intercepted her at the threshold.

"Oh goodness, what do you want from me?" she groaned.

The cat must have sensed Elaine's weakening resolve, because it chose that moment to wedge itself between her legs, cuddle snugly between her ankles, and lie down.

"Go back to your family. I'm sure they miss you." Elaine knelt down to pet the cat. No collar to be found and the poor creature was skin and bones. She ran a hand over its ribs and felt every single one. "Oh no. Do you have a family?"

The cat looked up at her and blinked slowly. Elaine was convinced she recognized something familiar in its eyes: loneliness.

Without another thought, Elaine scooped up the cat and carried it inside with her.

"I'll take you to the vet to see if you have a microchip or anything else, but, if not… well, you can stay with me for a little while. If they're gonna kick one of us out, we might as well stick together until that happens."

Elaine knew the cat didn't know what she was saying. And even if it did, it couldn't exactly hold her to her word. But still, it felt like Elaine was making an important promise. A vow.

In answer, the cat nestled against her chest and purred contentedly.

2

NEXT MORNING AT THE BEACH

Back in the old days, breakfast was sacred in the Robbins household. John would burn the toast while Elaine ravaged the eggs. Even when they were both still working, they'd wake up before the sun to make breakfast together. Then they'd carry their plates out to the patio and eat as the sun rose. It was the best part of Elaine's day.

Now, she still woke up early, but she got out of the house as soon as she could. She threw on some clothes, grabbed a granola bar and a travel mug of coffee, and left for a long walk.

At least a few days a week, she passed Charlene on the beach and they stopped to talk. But now that Charlene had adopted her grandson Tyler, it happened less often. Four-year-olds didn't exactly stick to schedules. Elaine didn't have children of her own, but she knew that much.

Still, she went out for her walk each day hoping to see the two of them playing on the beach. Hoping they'd have a few minutes to chat. Today, though, Elaine found Charlene's sister, Annette, sitting in the sand by herself.

"No bike ride today?" Elaine asked.

Annette looked up and grimaced. "Nope. My OB officially asked me to stop riding. Apparently, with my 'changing center of gravity,' I could fall and hurt the baby."

"Oh drat. That makes sense, but I'm sorry."

"Thanks," Annette grumbled. "Riding my bike is the only thing that has kept me sane this last year. I'm a little worried about how I'll cope without it."

"I get it, believe me," Elaine said. "That's what these morning beach walks are for me."

"At least you have a quiet house to go back to. I can't even meditate. You don't know what it's like to live with a house full of little boy noise."

"Unfortunately, I don't." She regretted the words as soon as she said them.

Even more so when Annette turned to her, eyes wide in horror.

"I'm sorry, Elaine. I didn't think."

"No, don't worry. It's fine. I didn't—"

"My filter is nonexistent these days," Annette stammered. "I blame pregnancy. Foot in mouth. I didn't even think about John and your house and—oh God, I'm making it worse. I'm sorry."

"It's fine," Elaine said calmly. "I didn't mean anything by it. Y'all just seem to have a lot of fun together. That's all I meant, dear."

"Are you sure? I'd hate it if you were upset with me."

"I'm really not upset, I promise."

Annette sighed. "It might be safest to stay away from me for the next nine months. These hormones are—woof. They're a lot. I feel a little crazy."

"Nonsense. You're a peach, as always." Elaine sat down on the sand next to Annette. "But speaking of living with your sister and Tyler... when are you moving out?"

Annette puffed a strand of hair out of her face. "Well, Noah will be moving in soon. And with the baby coming, I'd like to be out of their way as soon as possible."

"Oh my, so it's happening fast. Charlene told me she expected you to stay until after the baby was born."

"Yeah, she told me I could stay as long as I needed. But no one wants a newborn waking them up all hours of the night. Especially if the newborn in question isn't yours." Annette tried to smile, but it was a little too thin and feeble to be convincing.

"Feeling a little overwhelmed?"

Annette sagged. "Is it that obvious?"

"Well, only if the person you're talking to can see your face."

"Good to know," she sighed. "I'll be sure to only talk to Charlene through doors and over the phone. At least until I find something in my price range. Something *livable* in my price range."

"I understand that, too," Elaine said. "It can be expensive around here. Especially for a woman on her own."

Annette nodded. "Yeah. Frederick offered to help cover whatever I need, but I don't want him to have to do that."

"I'd say you should take the help where you can get it." Elaine didn't love asking for help, either, but she saw a good deal of it in her future. Since the bank wouldn't help, she was reaching the end of her rope.

"I will if I have to, but it's a last resort. He's only doing it because he feels guilty about cheating on me. And, I mean, he should feel guilty; I know that. But I don't want him to try to buy my forgiveness. I already forgave him, you know? It feels a little like taking his money would be, I dunno… reneging on that, sort of."

"You're a better person than me, that's for sure. I'm not sure I could do it."

Some days, Elaine still found herself upset with John for dying, as if it had been his choice. Cheating would be a whole 'nother kind of heartbreak, far beyond the pale.

"What do they say about grudges?" Annette asked. "Something about poison…"

"It's like taking poison and hoping the other person dies."

Annette snapped her fingers. "Exactly. That one. I don't want to do that, so I've forgiven him. I'm moving on. I don't want his money."

Elaine turned towards the water. The sun was coloring the ocean sherbet orange. *Moving on*—she'd thought about that more than a few times. Maybe things would feel easier if she started over the way Annette had.

Talking to her now, though, it seemed like maybe that wasn't necessarily a real solution. The past was like a shadow, trailing right along with you wherever you went.

"Okay, so maybe you don't take Frederick up on his offer. But I still don't think you should keep any of this from your sister," Elaine suggested. "Charlene would want to know if you were struggling."

Annette turned to Elaine and grabbed her hand. "Please don't tell her we talked about this."

"She's been through a lot the last few years, too. She'd want to help."

"Please," Annette begged. "I know the two of you talk about everything, but… I don't want her to know. She is so happy—with Noah moving in and Tyler doing well. I don't want her to feel guilty about my situation. It shouldn't be her problem."

Elaine sighed and zipped her fingers across her lips. "Silent as the grave."

"Thank you."

"I will just say that I think you're wrong about keeping this secret, but I'll stay quiet. It's not my business. Besides, who would I tell?"

"Charlene!" Annette laughed. "That's what I'm worried about."

"Who *else* would I tell, I mean. The only living creature at my house is a cat."

"A cat? Since when?"

"Last night. The poor little thing showed up at my doorstep, no collar or nothing."

"And you let it in?" Annette wrinkled her nose.

Elaine was still surprised herself. She'd never had a pet. Not growing up, nor as an adult. This stray was a first. But how could she explain it? *It seemed lonely, and I sensed a kindred spirit.* No, no, no. She was not going to turn into the widowed, lonely, crazy cat lady.

"It was half-starved and begging to come inside," she explained. "I felt bad for it. I'm taking it to the vet later today to see if it has a microchip."

"Have the vet check for fleas, too."

"Oh goodness, I didn't even think of that."

All Elaine could picture now was the cat curled up on the foot of her bed all night. She shuddered and shoved the thought aside. Too late to worry about that, she supposed.

"Anyway, the point is, my only roommate is a cat who can't talk. So rest assured, I won't tell." Suddenly, Elaine had a thought. "Hey!"

Annette jumped. "Um... hey?"

"Hey," Elaine said again, grabbing Annette's arm. "I don't have a roommate."

Annette narrowed her eyes. "Yeah, I know."

"I don't have a roommate, and you need a place to stay."

"Oh no." Annette shook her head. "I don't want to put you out, Elaine. You're so sweet, but this is my mess, and—"

"I've been planning to turn the house into a boarding house or a bed and breakfast or something, anyway."

"Well, yeah," Annette said, "I know, but… I don't know."

"I do," Elaine said. "You wouldn't be putting me out. You'd actually be *helping* me out."

"That's what you say now. But—"

"But nothing! I wouldn't offer if I didn't want you to accept. I may be nice, but I'm not that nice."

"Yes, you are." Annette took a deep breath. "I hate this."

Elaine patted her shoulder. "Asking for help isn't a weakness. It's a strength."

"That's what people say, but it's hard to feel that way when you're the one always asking for help." Annette peeked over at her. "Can I have time to think about it?"

"Of course. Take all the time you need. Whenever you're ready, I have an empty room with your name on it."

Turns out, rooms get dusty when you never use them.

Elaine stood in the doorway of the "ocean room" and remembered how excited she'd been to decorate it once upon a time.

"I wish this room had the master bathroom," she'd said. "It has the best view."

John had laughed. "Oh yeah. That little sliver of ocean visible over the rooflines. Look at us, living in luxury."

"It's luxury to me," she'd said.

Now, she couldn't remember the last time she'd been in there. Or, for that matter, the last time she'd been in any of the other rooms on this floor. Most of the second story was empty, so there was no reason to take the hike up the stairs.

"We'll buy furniture for them and decorate when the kids come along," John had said when they first moved in. "For now, we handle things one room at a time."

The problem was, the kids never came along.

Eventually, John turned one of the rooms into a model room. He hung model cars and motorcycles and planes from specialty shelves on the walls. He had a desk with a task lamp attached to it for extra light while painting and gluing small pieces together.

"You could have a hobby room, too," he'd encouraged her. "Maybe take up quilting or scrapbooking."

Elaine had wrinkled her nose. "No, thank you."

"Then how 'bout a library? Or a terrarium? Hang heat lamps and fill it with iguanas."

"Ew," she'd laughed. "No, I'd rather keep them empty."

The desire for children had come and gone—doubly so once John was gone, too. But the rooms had sat empty for long enough.

It was time to fill them.

First things first, though, she'd have to empty them of junk. A broken antique standing lamp, the old bedside tables she and John had taken out of their room and replaced years earlier, and half a dozen other lopsided forgettables stood mired in an ocean of dust.

"This is not fit for a baby," she muttered to herself. "Not fit at all."

Before she could set to work, however, she felt a soft coat brush against her leg. She looked down to see the nameless cat circling her ankles.

"Well, hello there. Does this mean you've finally forgiven me?"

The cat had been hiding under the living room sofa all afternoon, avoiding her. First, for neglecting to set out food before leaving for her walk, and second, for the vet visit.

On the first count, Elaine didn't have a choice. Unless she wanted to feed the cat chicken scraps and milk like she had the night before, she had to wait until the store opened so she could go buy actual cat food. Considering the animal had clearly been living outside for days, maybe weeks, Elaine assumed an extra hour or two before being fed in the morning wouldn't be a problem.

She was very wrong about that, however. When she'd walked through the door with the bag of cat food, the cat was lying in the center of the kitchen floor, howling up a storm.

As for the vet part, that was also non-negotiable. If she was going to let this thing stick around for any length of time, she needed to rule fleas out of the equation.

Thankfully, aside from being a bit thin, the cat had been sent home with a clean bill of health and a grudge against Elaine for her part in the affairs.

"Such a drama queen," she tutted. "Or drama king, rather." The vet had let her know the sex of the animal as well. She still didn't have a name for him, but that felt a bit like rushing things. She was just giving him a place to stay for now, that's all. No need to get so intimate.

He meowed and purred as he rubbed his head against her. Elaine bent down to give him a scratch between the ears.

"I'm glad we've mended fences. I've been worried sick over our fight," Elaine teased.

The cat purred into her palm.

"You're too friendly to be feral," Elaine remarked as she scooped the cat up. "You must have people out there who love you, no?"

There'd been no sign of a microchip when the vet had checked. No tags or collar, either. With no other options, the vet's office had offered to post some "Missing Cat" flyers in the office and on some message boards online.

"We have a lot of success with the message boards," the receptionist had mentioned. "Way more effective than signs on light posts. If anyone is looking for that cat, I bet we'll find 'em."

The thought twisted Elaine's stomach. It hadn't even been a full twenty-four hours, and she was already getting used to the furry company. But she couldn't outright refuse to look for the owners. That was a bridge too far towards selfish, she thought.

But for once in her life, Elaine *wanted* to be selfish. She squeezed the cat a little tighter. "You're happy here, aren't you, little one?"

Suddenly, the cat thrashed like it had been electrocuted, shimmying back and forth to try and get away from her.

"Alright, alright, I hear you!" As soon as Elaine relaxed her hold, the cat fell out of her arms and landed on his feet. He glared back at her, his green eyes glimmering with disgust. "So you can whine until I carry you around the house, but cuddling is off limits?"

He sauntered away with a swish of his tail.

Elaine snorted. "Grouchy little thing."

Once he was gone, she turned back to the empty room. She had some work to do before she could even think about charging anyone to live in these rooms. But at least she was starting with a blank slate.

With any luck, it wouldn't be blank for long.

3

NEXT DAY AT ISLE OF PALMS CITY HALL

Elaine paused at the base of the ramp and adjusted her blouse. Going business formal was probably overkill for a casual meeting at City Hall. It would just be a matter of regulations and filing the right paperwork. But after her bad luck at the bank, she wasn't taking any chances.

Elaine lifted her chin and practiced her smile. "I'm confident. I'm ready for this," she whispered. Then she glanced towards the crystal-clear blue sky. "Wish me luck, John."

She still wore a smile as she walked through the front doors. It was a small building. The entryway was little more than a central breezeway that branched off to different departments. A directory hanging on the wall to the right informed her she was looking for *Office 106 - Planning and Zoning.*

Suddenly, a throat cleared behind her. "Can I help you find something?"

She spun around. "Thank you, but I'm just heading to the—oh, Mason?"

The gray-bearded man in front of her grinned. "It can't be! Elaine Robbins? I haven't seen you in—Well, in a long time."

Since before John died. Elaine could tell he was thinking it, but he didn't want to bring up a sore subject. Not just sore for her, but for him, too. Mason and John had been good friends.

"A very long time," she agreed. "How have you been? How is Judy?"

"We've been fine. Working, eating, sleeping. The usual." He shrugged. "But we did just get back from visiting the kids in New Mexico. We stopped at Carlsbad Caverns while we were in the area."

"Are you still trying to visit every national park?"

He nodded. "Sure are. We're getting close, too. Only six more to go."

"Last time I saw Judy, I think you still had twenty left. You've been busy!"

"We try to hit one every season. At least every four months. Now that the kids are scattered to the wind, we can usually squeeze one in on the way to go visit."

Mason and Judy had four kids. Elaine had met Judy when she was still pregnant with their fourth, Alyssa.

"Alyssa is out of the house now, too? I guess that makes sense." Elaine shook her head. "But it seems impossible."

"You're telling me. I read somewhere that the days with kids are long, but the years are short," Mason said. "I thought I couldn't wait until we were empty-nesters, but now the house feels so quiet."

"Sure, sure." Elaine could relate all too well.

"But we've always loved to travel. Gets easier when we don't have to work around school schedules."

"A silver lining, for sure. Now you can gallivant around, knowing you raised some wonderful kids. You've earned the vacation."

He smiled. "Thanks. It keeps us busy."

"Because you two were never busy before?" Elaine teased. "I seem to remember your house being the watering hole for our little group."

Mason ran a hand over his beard. "Yeah. It still is, really. Judy is having the girls over for book club tomorrow. Murders and… No. What's it called?"

"Mysteries & Margaritas?"

"Yeah, that," he said. "You used to come over for that, didn't you?"

"I did." Elaine's face flushed. "I haven't been reading so much lately. I kind of… hit pause on book club, I guess."

Elaine had hit pause on most things when John died. But she would have quit Mysteries & Margaritas book club eventually, regardless. No one ever read the books and Elaine always got roped into being the designated driver just because she didn't hammer back margarita after margarita the way everyone else did.

"I get it. Life gets busy. I never read. Who has the time? With work and… other things." He chuckled. "Guess I'm just not much of a reader."

"Speaking of, what are you doing here?" Elaine asked. "I thought you worked in Charleston."

"I did, but I quit the firm a couple years ago. Now you're looking at the director of the Planning and Zoning Department for the Isle of Palms."

"Oh, wow!"

"Yes, it's very important," he laughed. "I spend my days telling people how far away from their property line they can install their pools. I just got off the phone with someone who wanted a two-story shed *in his front yard.*"

"You're kidding."

He lowered his voice a couple gravelly octaves. *"This is the land of the free, isn't it? How can I be free but can't build on my own property?"* Mason snorted. "Somedays, I feel like an elementary school teacher or something. I'm teaching people how to have basic courtesy for their neighbors."

"What would somebody even do with a two-story shed?"

"Block their neighbor's views and create an eyesore." He sighed. "I sound ungrateful. It's just been a long morning."

"Hopefully, I don't make it any longer." He frowned and Elaine pointed over her shoulder to the directory. "I'm looking for the Planning and Zoning Department. That would be you, Mr. Director?"

"Right! I almost forgot you were here for business. Sorry. Come with me."

The office was behind the first door on the left. A wooden counter ran from one wall to the other, splitting the square room in half. The three employees behind the desk looked up when the door opened, but quickly went back to whatever they'd been doing when they saw Mason had the situation under control.

"We can go into my office." Mason pointed to a door in the back corner. "Right through there."

The office was another square room, but much smaller. The walls were covered in National Parks posters—large, framed prints with candid pictures of Mason and Judy at the park tucked into the bottom corner.

"It looks great in here."

"Judy decorated it when I got the job," he said, almost sheepishly. Then he sat down behind his desk and folded his hands. "Okay. Down to business. What can I do for you?"

"Well," Elaine pulled out her folder and sat it in front of her on his desk, "I'm looking to rent out some rooms in my house. Hoping to earn a little extra money. And I'm wondering about permits I might need."

"You're looking for renters?"

Elaine could see realization dawn. It was like he was doing the math in his head. *Elaine − John + one big house = empty rooms.* She didn't know why, exactly, but she felt embarrassed.

"Yes. I'm hoping to make a little extra money, and I have the space, so—"

"Then you may want to speak with a real estate broker instead," he offered. "They could write up a basic rental contract for you. Handle the leasing and all that. I can help if you're looking to do big renovations. But otherwise—"

"Oh, no," she shook her head. "Sorry. I don't want roommates. I'm thinking about renting the rooms out for just a few days, a weekend, maybe a week or two. Like, a boarding house. Or a bed and breakfast."

His eyebrows rose. "You're starting a business?"

"I suppose so." Even though Elaine knew it would be a business in every way that mattered, it felt presumptuous to call it one already. All she had was extra space and an idea. Hardly a business.

"Well, then you'll want to go to the courthouse. That's where you'd apply for a business license."

"I'm not explaining this very well," she said. "I don't want it to be a business *business*. I'm thinking, like… have you ever used those online rentals? Where people post ads online and you can rent out their guesthouse or guest room for however long you need?"

He nodded. "We rented a tiny home in Arizona last summer. Hotter than the dickens with just a window A/C. But cheaper than a hotel. And Megan rents out her apartment from time to time on some site online."

"That's what I want to do," Elaine said. "Just a way for me to use my extra space and make a little money. But I don't know if I need any specific permits or permissions for that."

Mason stared at Elaine for a few seconds, his forehead creased. "Well, you might need a Short-Term Rental permit. I'd have to look into it. I don't deal with this too often. So, I'll do some research. Are you sure about this?"

Elaine blinked. "About the permits? No, that's why I came—"

"No," Mason said. He leaned forward. "I mean... renting out rooms? To strangers? It doesn't seem very safe."

"I think there is a vetting process online. A questionnaire. A background check, maybe. And I can refuse people if they don't seem up to snuff."

"But you can't always tell who is dangerous from a few questions online." His mouth flattened into a stern line. "I don't like it."

It didn't matter what Mason liked. She'd come for permits, not his permission.

"You said your daughter rents her apartment out."

He waved a hand dismissively. "Yeah, but Megan has Garrett."

Ah, there it was. Megan had a man in her life. Whereas Elaine was all alone.

"I know it's not exactly my business, but if anything happened to you. Well... I'd never forgive myself for not speaking my mind. And John wouldn't forgive me, either."

John would be proud of Elaine. She knew that much. He'd want her to move on and figure out her next steps.

"I've taken care of myself just fine the last three years, thanks."

Mason's neck flushed and he shifted in his chair. "I should have—" He cleared his throat. "When John died, we didn't stay in touch. *I* didn't stay in touch. With you. And I'm sorry for that."

Elaine shook her head. "I'm not trying to make you feel guilty, Mason. I'm just saying, I've done alright by myself so far. You don't need to worry."

"But I do," Mason insisted. "I do worry. After everything happened with John, Judy and I thought we'd give you space. But we should have been there for you. We should have checked in to make sure things were okay. I told John I would... if anything ever happened..."

Elaine could feel her throat tightening. She was burning up with embarrassment.

"I'm a grown woman, Mason. It's sweet that you're worried, but you... You're not obligated to look after me."

"Aren't I? John was too optimistic to actually think anything bad would happen. It was mostly just a joke. But we promised each other we'd always look out for each other. That included our families."

"That's nice, but—"

"If it had been me who had the heart attack—" He looked up at the ceiling and blinked. He was definitely fighting off emotion, if not tears. "If I'd been the one to pass, John would have looked after Judy and the kids, no question. I'm not as good of a man as he was. I haven't kept my promise the last few years. But you showing up here is a sign."

Elaine sighed. "Listen, Mason, you're very kind. But what I need right now isn't someone to worry about me or protect me. Or condescend to me."

"I'm not trying to—"

"I know you aren't," Elaine interrupted. "But I've had enough worry and fear in my life since John left. I don't need any more of it from anyone else."

And she definitely didn't need anyone in her life who was only there because they felt guilty.

His brows pinched together. "What do you need, then?"

"Information about permits," she said with a tight smile. "That's why I came here."

Mason held up his hands in surrender. "Okay, okay. You're right. I'm sorry. I'll look into it and give you a call."

"Thank you."

Before she walked through the door, Mason called after her. "Don't be a stranger."

Her eyes went slightly misty. It was too late for that.

4

LATE AFTERNOON AT ELAINE'S HOUSE

Elaine flipped the chicken thighs in the pan, smiling at their perfect caramelization. She just needed to brown the other side and then she could deglaze the pan with chicken broth.

"Five minutes for the chicken, twenty for the rice, twenty more minutes in the oven," Elaine muttered to herself as she did the math in her head. "Everything will be done at... carry the one... five-thirty."

She pulled out her phone and texted Annette and Charlene in a group chat.

I'll stop by with dinner at 5:40.

After her meeting at City Hall, Elaine had gone for another walk. She didn't usually double up, but her meeting with Mason had left her feeling restless. On her way home, she swung by Charlene's house.

"I wish I could chat, but Tyler is just getting over being sick," Charlene had said through the cracked doorway. "I'd invite you in, but—"

That explained why they hadn't been at the beach the past two mornings. "No, I completely get it. Don't worry about it."

Charlene sagged against the door frame. "His fever is mostly gone, but he won't sleep unless I'm next to him. And the kid has some very bony knees and elbows. I basically got pummeled all night. I don't think I slept more than thirty minutes."

"I'm so sorry. What can I do to help? I can make a grocery store run. What if I cook you all dinner?"

"Well…"

"I won't take no for an answer," Elaine insisted. "I'll text you before I head over."

Now, her kitchen was a disaster in the best way.

"Can you believe I'm cooking?" she asked John. "You probably thought I forgot how."

It was hard to justify cooking on a regular basis when most of the ingredients would just go to waste before she could use them. Takeout was easier.

Thank you!!!!!!! Annette responded.

A message from Charlene followed: *Seriously. Thank you!*

Elaine was still smiling at the messages when an unknown number flashed on her screen. She wasn't in the habit of answering unknown calls, but mostly because she wasn't in the habit of answering many phone calls at all. She didn't have too many people chomping at the bit to talk to her.

After a brief pause, she swiped up. "Hello?"

"Hey, Elaine. It's Mason."

"Oh. Hey there." She checked the number again. "Are you calling from your work phone?"

"No. It's my cell."

She would've assumed his number was in her phone, but thinking back, Mason always called John. Even when they all got together—the men and Elaine and Judy, too—John and Mason arranged it. Elaine didn't even know if she had Judy's number. Book club meetings were scheduled through email.

"Elaine? Can you hear me?" he asked.

"Yeah, sorry. What's going on?"

"Just wanted to follow up on what we talked about today. I looked into your situation and you'll need to submit a Short-Term Rental application, but that's it."

"An application? Does that mean I have to be approved?" Her heart clenched. Every bank she'd been to had practically laughed in her face. She couldn't stand another rejection.

He hummed noncommittally. "Technically, yes. But almost everyone is accepted. It's more of a formality. Just a way for the city to know where rental properties are located. As long as you aren't trying to rent out a condemned building or cram forty people in a studio apartment, you'll be fine."

She sighed in relief. "I don't plan to do either of those things."

"Perfect. Text me your email, and I'll send you the application. You can fill it out and send it back to me when you're done."

"Thank you so much, Mason. You've been a big help."

"Of course. My pleasure," he said. There was a brief pause before he let out a sigh. "I know what you said this morning, but I just have to say one more time… be careful. Please."

"I will."

"I don't want to be condescending or however you said it. But I want to make sure you're safe," he said. "Would you—would it be a problem for you if I stopped by every so often? Once you get the rooms rented out, I mean? I'd like to see you a bit more often. Make sure you're alive and well over there."

"You don't need to do that," Elaine started to say. How many times did she need to let this man off the hook before he'd finally leave it be?

"I know I don't have to. I want to," he said quickly.

Elaine wanted to refuse. She didn't want to be on anyone's chore list. But then again… if he wanted to…

"Um, okay. Sure," she said. "You certainly don't have to go to all the trouble, but if you'd like to—"

"Great. Judy will be glad to hear that."

Elaine frowned. "She will?"

"I talked to her after you left this morning. She suggested it, actually. Apparently, the book club gals have asked about you. Everyone's been worried."

How worried could they have been if they never bothered to reach out and check?

"But I'll be sure to keep in touch. Make sure everything is going well. For you *and* for John."

At this point, it would be easier to agree than argue. So she thanked him as briefly as she could and hung up.

Elaine checked the time and yelped. She was running late. The back side of the chicken had gotten a bit darker than she'd wanted, but it was still fine. She lifted it out of the pan and poured in the chicken broth. The pan sizzled and spit hot butter and chicken fat, which Elaine dodged.

When she turned to grab the rice off the counter, she nearly tripped over the cat.

"What are you doing underfoot?" she asked, toeing gently at the little beast's soft underbelly. "You're going to get squashed."

He licked the floor where a bit of fat had splattered.

"Ah. You got a taste for chicken the other day, didn't you? Well, this isn't for you, I'm afraid."

She stepped over him and the naughty little thing made a playful swipe at her ankle.

"Violence is never the answer, you know."

Elaine poured the rice into the simmering water, placed the chicken back on top, and then slid the entire cast iron skillet into the oven. When she turned around, the cat was pawing pitifully at its face, purring loudly.

"I won't give you chicken, but I'll give you scratches." She dropped down to the floor and the cat crawled slowly into her lap. "There you go, Mister."

Elaine pulled back and looked at the little black and white face staring up at her. "Hey, do you want a name?"

Green eyes blinked back at her.

"I bet you do. Everyone needs a name. Temporary or not." She scratched behind his ears and his eyes rolled back in his head with pleasure.

"I'll take that as you agreeing with me." She narrowed her eyes and stared back, trying to get a sense for who the little monster was. But nothing came to her. "I'll think on it and get back to you."

She could hear John warning her against it. *"If you name that little monster, you'll never be able to let it go."*

He was probably right. But John also would have told her to slam the back door in the starving cat's face. He wasn't right about everything.

When her oven timer went off, Elaine jumped up from the floor, earning her a displeased yowl from the cat.

"Drama king," she said as he skulked away under the dining room table.

He just flicked his tail in response.

Fifteen minutes later, Elaine was walking up Charlene's and Annette's front walk with the meal neatly portioned in travel-safe dishes. "Sorry I'm late."

Annette waved her away. "Ten minutes after is on time by my standards. Besides, you come bearing gifts. All is forgiven."

Elaine handed over the food containers. Annette immediately cracked them open and took a whiff. "Oh goodness. All is absolutely forgiven."

"How's Tyler doing?" Elaine asked.

"Much better!" Charlene said. "He took a nap this afternoon without me sleeping next to him."

"Only because I was sleeping next to him," Annette interjected. "But still, it's progress."

"Well, he's lucky to have the two of you looking after him. I just wish I could do something to help."

"That's the joy of being the neighbor and not the parent—"

"Or the aunt," Annette added.

"You don't have to deal with the bodily fluids," Charlene finished.

"You have a point," Elaine said. "But I've missed seeing you two on the beach. I look forward to it every day."

Charlene groaned. "I've missed it, too. Being locked inside with a sick kid has me feeling crazy. I've watched the same movie three times today."

"I know all the words to every single song on the soundtrack," Annette added.

Elaine felt bad for them. But even having family around to complain about seemed like a luxury.

"Poor kiddo," Elaine said. "And poor you two. Sounds like you both need some kid-free time soon."

Annette clapped. "That's it! Girls' night!"

Charlene and Elaine looked at one another. "Huh?"

"Girls' night," Annette repeated. "The three of us, a bottle of wine, maybe some cheese."

"I think you're forgetting my sick kid," Charlene said. "And your kid. You're pregnant."

"Oh, right. No wine for me. But I can have sparkling juice. And Noah can take care of Tyler for a night, right?"

Elaine's heart swelled. "That sounds fun."

"It does, but…" Charlene wavered. "I don't know. I'd feel bad sending Tyler to Noah's if—"

"Noah is going to live here soon enough," Annette cut in. "It's about time he earned his keep."

Charlene laughed. "He doesn't need to earn anything, Annie."

"Maybe not, but Noah takes care of Tyler on his own all the time. He won't mind. You need a break." Annette squeezed Charlene's shoulder. "We both do. Desperately."

"Me too!" Elaine added.

Annette turned to her. "Is your rescue cat sick? Is that what you need a break from?"

Truthfully, Elaine needed a break from the loneliness. But she wasn't going to say that out loud, of course.

"Cat?" Charlene asked.

"That cat is fine," Elaine said. "But I still need a girls' night. It's been too long since we've all had time to sit and chat."

"Can we chat about how you have a cat now?" Charlene asked. "How did I not know this?"

"I didn't see you on my walk the last two mornings, so—"

Annette jumped between them. "Save it for girls' night. We don't want to run out of stuff to talk about."

"We won't run out of stuff to talk about. And it's not a long story," Elaine said. "The cat was—"

"Shhh," Annette insisted. "Save it for tomorrow. Seven o'clock."

Charlene pinched the bridge of her nose and shook her head. "Sorry about my sister."

"Sorry about *my* sister," Annette shot back.

"Y'all have nothing to apologize for," Elaine laughed. "I'll see you both tomorrow."

5

THE NEXT EVENING AT ELAINE'S HOUSE

"What even happens at a girls' night?" Elaine pondered out loud to John as she tied her wrap dress into a bow at her hip. "Annette said something about wine. I can do that."

She looked down at herself. The bow hung limp and lopsided like a wilting flower. She undid it and tried again.

"Maybe we'll watch a movie?" Elaine looked up at John's face smiling out from the frame. "But I'd be okay with just chatting, too. I don't have much to say, but still."

Just being around other people would be nice. Her house felt like a vacuum sometimes, silent and empty.

"I can tell them about my chat with Mason." Elaine chuckled darkly. "I know you like him, but Annette is going to have a real bone to pick with him. I mean, maybe you did ask him to look after me—which we'll talk about later—but did he have to act like it was such a chore?"

Her face flushed just thinking about it. "It was embarrassing, for crying out loud. He treated me like I was some shut-in. I won't be surprised if they drop by to make sure I haven't slipped in the tub or fallen down the stairs."

The bow on her dress looked clumsy no matter how hard she tried. After a few more attempts, Elaine gave up with a groan and changed into white jeans and a loose denim shirt.

She smoothed her shirt and smiled up at John's photograph on the bureau. "Better."

He smiled back, but it didn't reach his eyes. For a man who smiled for so much of his life, Elaine had never been able to capture that smile in a picture. The John smile, the real one, the crinkly-eyed grin he made when he was belly laughing.

A tear streaked down her cheek and Elaine swiped it away. "No, no. Not tonight," she snapped to herself. "I'm late enough as it is."

The cat, still nameless, slunk out of his hiding spot on top of the fridge. Curious green eyes watched her. Elaine got the sense he was worried.

"I'm fine," she sniffled. "Go back to sleep. I'll be home later."

He watched her anyway as she grabbed her purse. She reached over and scratched his head. "Don't wait up."

"I didn't consider the implications of being pregnant on girls' night." Annette frowned into her glass of sparkling grape juice.

"I reminded you yesterday when you came up with the idea. And wine always gives you a headache, anyway." Charlene topped off her glass and headed into the living room. "You'll feel better than all of us tomorrow."

Annette snorted. "My constant nausea, heartburn, and exhaustion would like a word with you."

"All part of the price you pay for a baby. But we aren't pregnant, so…" Charlene leaned over the coffee table and clinked glasses with Elaine.

"Oh yeah, you two cheers it up," Annette griped. "I'll be over here with my juice box."

Charlene laughed. "Sorry, Elaine. I had no idea we'd be in such bitter company tonight."

"No one needs to apologize to me for anything," Elaine said. "Be as bitter as you want, Annette. You've earned it. I'm just glad to be here."

Elaine hadn't said much since she'd arrived. Charlene and Annette were more than entertaining on their own. She heard enough of her own voice at home as it was. It was nice to listen to someone else chatter for a change.

"Thank you, Elaine." Annette cast a pointed look at her sister. "Someone understands the spirit of the festivities."

"I thought it was to get together and enjoy each other's company," Charlene said.

"No. It's where we go to complain about our problems. To a chorus of sympathetic voices, obviously," Annette said.

"Why not both?"

Annette lifted her glass of juice. "A toast to compromise."

"To good company and complaints."

Charlene sighed and raised her glass to join the others. "Fine. If we're complaining, I'll start."

"If you complain about me, I'm kicking you out of the house," Annette warned.

"You took care of Tyler last night, and I got six straight hours of sleep. You're a goddess amongst mortals and I wouldn't dream of complaining about you," Charlene said. "My complaint is about my current flip. We are way behind schedule. I should be finishing the decorating and staging by now, but we are still dealing with sheet rock."

"I thought you had painters coming in a few days?"

"I do!" Charlene shook her head. "But this is the first time I've used this crew for sheet rock and they are slower than molasses."

"Can you ask for a discount?" Elaine asked. "To at least cover the cost of some of your trouble."

"They're taking a day of labor off the final price, which helps cover some of it. But I don't even really care about that. I'm just itching to decorate. It's the best part."

Annette clutched her heart. "Oh, Elaine. Have you seen this house yet? You should see it. It might be my favorite one she's ever done."

"I haven't." Elaine frowned. "I actually haven't seen any of your flips in person, Charlene. Just pictures online from when you list them."

"You're welcome to drop by anytime you want. Maybe after the sheet rock guys finish up... *If* they ever finish." Charlene sank into the couch.

"They'll finish," Annette encouraged her. "And when they do, it's going to be amazing. Show Elaine your sketches."

Charlene waved her hand. "No. No one wants to—"

"I do!" Elaine interrupted. "I'd love to see."

Annette was already off the couch and heading towards the table. She grabbed a large binder and flipped it open. "The drawings are pretty loose, but they give you a good idea. It's like—what would you call it, Charlene? I'd say it's kind of beachy. But a classy kind of beachy. Like—"

"It's coastal design," Charlene said. "Lots of blues, wood, and natural fabrics."

Annette handed Elaine the binder, and she flipped through the pages. There were hand drawn pictures of rooms with cutouts of furniture and paint swatches taped around the edges. It was exactly like they'd both described it: beachy, but a classy kind of beachy.

"These are great." Elaine slowly turned through the pages. "Do you do this with all of your flips?"

"I have to. If I don't make a binder with all of my ideas, I forget them. Or end up going way over budget. It helps to have a solid plan."

Was that Elaine's problem? Maybe she should try it with the bed and breakfast idea. It was a hard sell, though. She'd had a solid plan with John and that had gone to hell in a handbasket. Plans never seemed worth the trouble after that.

Elaine whistled. "I knew you flipped houses, but I never knew—Well, I just didn't realize... You are very talented, is what I'm trying to say. This looks gorgeous."

"It's just some rough mockups, but thanks," Charlene said. "Davy was better at a lot of the planning and scheduling than me, but I always took lead on the designs."

"I can certainly see why."

Annette leaned over Elaine's shoulder and sighed. "If I had the money, I'd buy the house myself. It's going to be amazing. All those windows."

Elaine nudged Charlene's leg. "Sounds like I need you to come decorate my house for me."

"Why? Your house is beautiful."

"I don't have a theme like this."

"Who cares?" Charlene said. "So long as there is some cohesion from room to room, theme doesn't matter. Your house is charming. Very comfortable."

"You're sweet, but it's a mish-mash. Mostly things we found at estate sales or family heirlooms. John's dad built our dining room table."

"That adds character," Annette said. "People love character."

"What about empty rooms?" Elaine asked. "How would you spin an empty room covered in dust—if you were trying to sell it?"

Annette narrowed her eyes in thought. "I'd say it was decorated in the Minimalist style."

Elaine laughed. "Yep. That settles it. I need you two on my team. Charlene on staging, Annette on sales."

"Are you officially doing that?" Charlene asked. "The bed and breakfast thing?"

"At least the bed thing. I'm not so sure about the breakfast just yet."

"If your breakfasts are anything like the chicken and rice you made last night, then you should definitely make breakfast," Annette said. "It was delicious. Well worth the heartburn I got."

"I'm glad you liked it. But I'm not sure if I'd need a different permit for that. I know I can rent out the rooms, but can I feed people? I'd have to ask Mason."

Annette and Charlene looked at each other, eyebrows raised.

"Mason?" Annette asked. "Who is that?"

Elaine knew what she was really asking. "He's married with four children."

"Oh."

"He works at the Planning and Zoning office," she continued. "He did some permit research for me."

"If you're already at the permit stage, then you must be pretty close to ready," Charlene said.

Elaine fought back a wince. "I wasn't kidding about the empty room. Or the dust. The house isn't ready at all."

"Were you kidding about us working for you?" Annette asked. "Because I'd love to help. I have a pretty nice camera. I can take photos for the listings and help with the sales pitch."

Charlene frowned at her sister. "You've never offered to take my listing photos."

Annette lifted her nose into the air and put on a fake haughty voice. "You can't afford me. But for Elaine, I'll work pro bono."

"Har de har har." Charlene rolled her eyes at her sister and then turned to Elaine. "But really, I'd love to help, too. Like I said, my project is stalled out right now and I'm itching to decorate."

"You are both so nice to offer, but I don't have much of a budget right now." She didn't have a budget to speak of, actually. If she opened her wallet, she was fairly certain moths would fly out. "I don't want to take your help and not pay you. It wouldn't be right."

"Are you serious?" Annette looked from Elaine to Charlene. "Is she serious?"

"I think she is," Charlene nodded solemnly.

Annette turned back to Elaine. "Do you remember when I found out I was pregnant? I was in shock and confused, trying to figure out what to do about Frederick and Gregory."

Elaine nodded. How could she forget?

"And do you remember how you practically held my hand and walked me towards the right decision?"

"Well, I mean... I wouldn't say it like that."

"I would," Annette said. "You've basically been my therapist since I've moved here. If anything, I owe you this."

Charlene hummed in agreement. "You do far too much free babysitting for me. I definitely owe you."

"I love Tyler," Elaine protested. "It's my pleasure."

"Regardless. We both want to help you out," Charlene said. "It's what friends do."

Friends. Elaine was almost embarrassed at the way the word rushed through her, a little electrical zip of energy she hadn't realized she needed.

She suppressed a smile and her urge to argue. "Well, then... when do we start?"

The Next Day At Lowcountry Resale

Charlene held up the receipt like she was planning to frame it. "I told you I could get you decorations on the cheap."

"I feel like we're stealing. Was this really only fifty dollars?" Elaine pushed a cart overflowing with pillows, throw blankets, and knickknacks through the front doors of the thrift store. It was a beautiful day, glowing and warm. It felt nice to be out on the town.

"Fifty dollars and thirty-nine cents." Charlene grinned like she'd just won the lottery. "What a thrill."

"You're a professional."

"Literally," Charlene laughed. "I stage all of the flip houses myself, so I have to be on the hunt for a good deal."

"I've never even heard of Lowcountry Resale before." The store was tucked away in the parking lot behind a church. If it hadn't been for Charlene, Elaine would have driven right past. It looked more like a storage facility.

"It's off the beaten path, but still one of my favorites. Especially when I'm looking for the finishing touches: pops of color and personality to catch buyers' eyes." She leaned over and whispered, "It also doesn't hurt that they give me a twenty percent discount."

"That's nice of them."

Charlene shrugged. "They aren't losing any money on me. I've spent more than enough here. Plus, I send a lot of business Dan and Emily's way. I've mentioned their store on countless online house flipping forums."

"Well, you've found them another customer. I'll be coming here again, that's for sure." A pillow bounced out of the cart and Elaine reached down to pick it up. "I mean, look at this pillow. No offense, but... it's kind of hideous."

"Offense taken," Charlene laughed.

"No, I mean—well, I meant what I said. It's hideous. But as soon as you said how great it would look with the pale blue walls—"

"Like a sunset," Charlene nodded. "The perfect color scheme for the ocean view room."

Elaine held the pillow up against the blue sky. "Now, it feels like I found the perfect piece. I'm so glad you're here. I just don't have the vision for this kind of thing. What did you call it?"

"Staging."

"Yes, that," Elaine said. "Staging has to be a marketable skill, right?"

"Definitely. House stagers cost a pretty penny. That's why Davy and I learned to do it ourselves. We saved a fortune."

"And now I'm saving a fortune. It feels like I'm cheating you. If you give me some kind of hourly rate or something, I'd be happy to—"

Charlene waved her away. "Nonsense. Friends and family discount, one hundred percent off."

Elaine really didn't like accepting favors. Especially since she had squat to offer in return. But before she could argue, someone stepped in front of their cart. Elaine barely stopped in time to avoid running over the woman's feet.

"I'd say I'm surprised to see you here, Charlene, but I'd be lying."

She was a short woman with black hair nearly longer than she was. And now that the cart was at a full stop, Elaine realized she recognized her. Usually, her long hair was twisted into a bun on top of her head, held in place by the pen she used to take orders at Front Beachtro. Elaine saw a lot of the woman. She was something of a regular.

Charlene grinned. "I'm predictable, I guess. How are you, Janie?"

Janie. Elaine tried to commit that to memory. She'd never been good with names.

"I'm alive, so it's a good day," Janie said. "I'm actually here to pick some things up for bridge night."

"What else could you possibly need?" Charlene turned to Elaine. "This woman is the host of all hosts. You think staging is a marketable skill? Her party planning abilities blow me out of the water."

"Oh hush, you're pouring it on thick."

"I'm not. I was serious about showing Gregory pictures from your *Alice in Wonderland* themed dinner a few months ago. Next time he comes to see Annette, I'm going to tie him down and make him appreciate your talents."

"Don't commit any felonies on my behalf," Janie said even as she beamed. "And that was just for fun."

"A party?" Elaine felt like she was in a play and had forgotten her lines. "Was it a birthday party or—"

"It was for our weekly bridge game," Charlene said. "One week out of the month, Janie hosts it and she doesn't do anything halfway. I mean, the muffins decorated like mushrooms and all the mismatched chairs like a Mad Hatter tea party—it was incredible."

"Bridge is a card game, right?" Elaine asked.

"Yeah, but only half of us know how to play. There's a lot of wine involved, too."

"Too much wine sometimes," Janie laughed. "Remember when Sarah fell into Rhonda's fish pond?"

Both women fell into hysterics. Elaine smiled and patiently waited for them to finish.

Charlene wiped her eyes. "When is it your turn to host again, Janie? Next week or—"

"The week after," Janie said. "I'm actually here looking for some old candelabras. Don't tell the other girls, but I'm working on a *Phantom of the Opera* theme for October."

Elaine perked up. "That's my favorite musical. Andrew Lloyd Webber is amazing."

Janie frowned. "I thought Gerard Butler played the phantom?"

"Oh, well, he did. In the movie," Elaine said. "But Andrew Lloyd Webber wrote the original musical. He's a composer."

"You're like a Wikipedia article. It must be your favorite," Janie smiled. "You're welcome to come if you want to—"

"Oh, I'm so rude!" Charlene patted Elaine's shoulder. "This is Elaine. Elaine, this is Janie."

"Nice to meet you," Elaine said. She didn't bother mentioning Janie had served her the breakfast platter at Front Beachtro the last three times she'd been in.

Janie nodded. "You too. You're welcome to come, Elaine. Despite how Charlene made it sound, it's a casual thing. Just a few gals from around town. Some I met while working at the bistro."

"Like me." Charlene posed with her hands under her chin.

"We haven't been open long, but we already have the best regulars."

Apparently, going for breakfast three times per week didn't make you a regular.

"But please, feel free to join us," Janie said. "Charlene can give you all the details. Hope to see you there!"

If she did, she probably wouldn't remember, Elaine thought bitterly.

After the women said their goodbyes, Charlene and Elaine walked to Elaine's car to unload.

"Janie is the greatest. You'll love her," Charlene said. "I'm actually surprised you two don't know each other already. You eat at the bistro sometimes, right?"

"Yeah. Weird," Elaine mumbled.

Charlene shrugged. "A case of a missed connection, I guess."

Or a faulty connection. It was starting to feel like the story of Elaine's life.

6

THE NEXT DAY AT ELAINE'S HOUSE

Elaine barely recognized her old house. Sunlight poured through the windows, bringing warmth to the new-to-her furniture and furnishings. It was hard to believe the rooms had been sitting empty less than twenty-four-hours earlier.

"Are you sure I can't give Noah anything for this bedframe?" Elaine asked Charlene. "It's in great condition."

The full-size bedframe was a warm mahogany with a matching headboard. It looked great with the original wood floors. And the cream rug they'd found at the thrift store softened the place up. It had been Charlene's idea to spray paint an old stool from the garage white to work as a bedside table.

"This frame was in his guest room, so no one was using it. It's basically brand new," Charlene said. "You did him a favor, though. He's trying to get rid of his extra stuff before we move in together."

Everyone was sacrificing to help Elaine out, but they kept saying *she* was doing *them* a favor.

Since Charlene's house flipping project was stalled, she was desperate to decorate. Elaine letting Charlene decorate her house for free was somehow a "favor."

Annette's camera had languished in her closet for almost a year, so utilizing her photography skills and natural talent for marketing was also a "favor."

"At this point, I feel like I could steal your wallet out of your purse, and you'd thank me for making it lighter for you," Elaine said. "Y'all are being too nice to me."

Annette padded in from the hallway, flipping through the pictures she'd just taken of the downstairs. "Too nice? Is there such a thing as 'too nice'?"

"Definitely not," Charlene said. "And even if there was, it would have to be a lot nicer than we've been the last two days. Like, donating both kidneys—*that* would be too nice."

Elaine shook her head. "I think you're underestimating how much you've helped me out. And how much money I've saved. Without you both, I would still be twiddling my thumbs over which pillow shams to buy. But thanks to you... I mean, look at this place."

Elaine actually couldn't stop looking at it. The rooms upstairs had been empty for so long, and Elaine had only ever imagined them in nursery greens or yellows, decorated with a crib and mobile. She'd assumed decorating them for the rentals would be bittersweet.

But seeing how elegantly everything had turned out, there was no bitterness at all. It was just sweet.

Annette spun around to the hallway. "Where is that darned cat?"

"What did he do?" Elaine asked.

"He's a ninja! I didn't see him when I was taking the pictures, but he's in every single one." Annette held out her camera. "Look!"

Elaine squinted to see the picture on the small screen. "Are you sure? I don't see him in—"

"Under the sofa."

Elaine looked to the shadows under the couch, and sure enough, a white splotch of fur and two green eyes were visible.

"It looks like he's going to pounce anyone who walks through the door. Not exactly welcoming," Annette sighed. "He's sabotaging you, Elaine."

Charlene grabbed the camera and flipped through the photos, laughing harder at each one. "He's literally in every single photo. How did you not see him move from under the sofa to on top of the refrigerator?"

Annette threw up her hands. "The cat is like a ghost, I'm telling you."

"Well, either way, it's not sabotage. It's charming," Charlene said. "Or it can be."

"Yeah, you're supposed to be my spin team, right? How would you sell a vaguely homicidal-looking cat to potential renters?"

Annette pursed her lips. "Well… I'd offer a prize to anyone staying here who can find the cat in every single photo."

Elaine laughed. "That's an amazing idea. I'll give them twenty-five dollars off the room."

"And if people like cats, he is cuddly from time to time. He let me rub his belly earlier."

"If they don't like cats?" Elaine asked.

"Then they'll never know he's here at all." Annette held up her camera. "The little ghost cat knows how to keep a low profile."

"Little ghost," Elaine mumbled. "Huh. Is that a name?"

"Is what a name?" Charlene asked.

"Ghost. I've been trying to come up with a name with him and nothing has felt right. But Ghost... I don't know, it has a certain ring to it."

Annette smiled. "I think it's perfect."

"So do I," Elaine said. "Then it's decided. Hear that, Ghost? Your name is Ghost!"

Suddenly, a black-and-white furball shot out from under the rocking chair. Annette shrieked and nearly dropped her camera on the floor.

"How did he get in here?" Annette growled.

Elaine and Charlene were laughing too hard to answer.

If having renters was going to be even a fraction as much fun as this, Elaine couldn't wait.

"Can I come up yet?" Elaine called from the base of the stairs. "I finished reading through the listing and the room descriptions fifteen minutes ago. It all looks great."

"I know it does," Annette yelled back. "That was just to distract you."

"From what?"

Elaine had been sequestered to the dining room an hour earlier. Annette and Charlene were being secretive and making a lot of noise. Elaine had no earthly idea what was going on.

"It's a surprise," Charlene said. "Give us five more minutes."

Elaine sighed and paced back into the dining room. All morning, she'd been so busy moving furniture, packing away personal items, and getting the rooms ready for potential renters that she hadn't had the chance to stop and think about what she was doing. About what she was *really* doing.

Inviting people into her home. Into the house she'd shared with John. The home where they'd planned out their life together. Where they'd experienced hopes and disappointments, highs and lows.

Bringing people into that space was a lot more personal than Elaine had imagined.

People would be renting a room from her, but they'd be walking through the halls she and John had painted after they'd moved in. They'd sit on the furniture where she and John had cuddled together to watch thrillers (his favorite) and romantic comedies (hers). Strangers would sit at the dining room table John's father had built as a wedding gift and look up at the framed picture of Elaine and John— the picture that had been Elaine's only company for the last several years.

Was she ready for that?

"Five more minutes," Annette called. "We are almost done."

Well, she'd have to figure out a way to get ready. She couldn't afford to drag her feet much longer.

It helped that they'd only set up one room so far. Baby steps. That's what Elaine needed right now. Maybe one day she'd have a proper boarding house with every room filled and she'd cook meals in big pots and pans in the kitchen and take care of folks.

But for right now, she needed an adjustment period. Living on her own for so long, lonely as it could be at times, would be a hard habit to break.

After a final bang upstairs, Elaine heard footsteps on the stairs. Then Charlene and Annette stood in the doorway, grinning.

"Come with us," Annette said.

Elaine followed them up the stairs. "What is going on?"

"I hope you don't mind, but we took a little initiative," Charlene said over her shoulder. "I know we only agreed to help you decorate and stage the one bedroom. But we love this idea and are so proud of you for taking the leap. So we wanted to surprise you with another one."

Charlene stopped outside John's model car room, and Elaine's heart squeezed.

She knew the day might come when she'd have to pack the models away. But that day wasn't today. Or this month. This year, even.

Elaine braced herself as Charlene pushed the door open. She was already preparing to lie to the women's faces about loving their surprise, all while planning to somehow return every single model to the wall where they belonged. She didn't want to hurt their feelings, after all. She'd simply undo whatever they'd done without making a fuss and—

Annette threw the door open. "Ta-da!"

The models were still on the walls. Every car, train, plane, and motorcycle was exactly where John had left them. Except now they sparkled.

"You dusted."

Annette laughed. "Out of everything, that's what you notice?"

It was. Elaine had been so sure the cars were going to be gone that seeing them still on the walls made it hard to look at anything else. But when she managed to pull her eyes away, she realized the room had been rearranged and redecorated.

"We had to move John's desk to make room for the bed," Charlene said. "I hope you don't mind."

His desk used to sit in front of the window, but now it was tucked neatly into the back corner. In its place was a full-sized bed with a white comforter tucked around the mattress.

"Where did you—?"

"Davy and I had this bedframe sitting in our attic for years. It was in rough shape, but I scrubbed it down last night. I think it looks pretty good."

Elaine gaped. "The mattress—"

"Is actually just a couple old folding tables with a comforter thrown over top," Annette finished. "You definitely can't lay on it right now. But we can photograph it and schedule it to be rented out. Fredrick is selling our old house in Asheville, and he promised I could have the mattresses from the guest room. He's planning to bring them up in the next few days along with some of my other stuff."

How would the girls spin this as Elaine doing them a favor? Because she didn't see any possible way. This was an outright gift.

"I don't—I can't accept this," she stammered.

"Of course, you can!" Charlene said. "It didn't cost us a penny to get this room ready for you."

"The walls are so colorful, the room practically decorated itself," Annette said. "The model cars are a little niche, but I can totally sell it. People like a themed room."

Elaine was lost for words. She didn't know how to tell them what she was thinking, what she was feeling. She hardly knew herself.

"Well?" Charlene prodded.

"Do you like it? Love it? Hate it?" Annette asked, rapid-fire.

"I—" Elaine shook her head. "It's so… I don't know how…"

Annette groaned. "You're actually killing me, Elaine."

"I love it," Elaine choked out. She was fighting to keep the tears at bay. "I love it so much. Downstairs, I was… I was packing bits and pieces of John away. And up here, you… you celebrated him."

All at once, she lost the fight. Tears rolled down her cheeks.

"Oh, Elaine." Charlene pulled her in for a hug. "We didn't mean to make you cry."

Elaine swiped at her eyes. "They're happy tears, I promise."

Annette joined the hug. "Are you sure? Because we can put it all back the way it was. I took pictures of the 'before' just in case."

"Don't touch a thing," Elaine said. "I love it."

"I'm so glad," Charlene said.

Elaine sniffled. "It's time for me to let go of him a little. Logically, I know John is gone. I know he doesn't live here anymore. But part of me, as embarrassing as it is to say, always imagined him coming back and being so pleased I'd kept things just like he'd left them."

Charlene shook her head. "That's not embarrassing. I did the same thing with Davy's stuff for a long time. I wasn't ready to move on."

Elaine gave them a watery smile. "I didn't think I was ready, either, but looking at this—it's perfect. It's everything John would have wanted."

"You're starting over and building a future for yourself, but you can still take a little bit of John with you," Annette said. "Matter of fact, you should."

Moving on didn't have to mean letting go. Not completely, anyway. And that was exactly what Elaine needed to hear.

She pulled them both close. "Thank you."

7

ONE WEEK LATER AT FRONT BEACHTRO

The mid-morning crowd at Front Beachtro was picking up, and Janie was the only server working. She slid a spinach and cheese omelet in front of Charlene, a ham and potato scramble in front of Elaine, and a Tiny Tot's stack of pancakes in front of Tyler.

"Enjoy your meal," she said. "Holler if you need anything."

"Thanks, Janie." Elaine smiled up at the woman the same way she had a dozen other times before. None of which had been too memorable, apparently, considering Janie hadn't remembered her.

"You're so welcome." Janie smiled back.

Elaine studied the smile, trying to see if Janie even remembered her from the other day at the thrift store. Maybe Elaine simply didn't make an impression. Maybe she had a forgettable face.

The waitress's smile was bland and friendly, though. It revealed nothing.

As soon as she walked away, Tyler let out a little holler. "Yeehaw!"

"Not that kind of holler." Charlene mussed his light brown hair. "Do you want syrup?"

"Yes."

"Yes what?"

He grinned with all of his teeth. "Pleeeeease."

Charlene spread his butter, drizzled on syrup, and cut the pancakes into thin strips to make them easier to eat. Only once Tyler was happily munching away did she turn to her own food with a sigh.

"Always keeping you busy, huh?" Elaine said.

"That's an understatement. But it's a fun kind of busy. Usually." She gave a weary smile. "It's good to get out of the house. Thanks for inviting us both out. I know hanging around with a mom and a little kid isn't—"

"It's wonderful," Elaine interrupted. "I love seeing you both. Even you, little troublemaker."

Tyler grinned up at her, syrup dripping down his chin.

"Still, thanks," Charlene lowered her voice. "A lot of people don't think to include him in our plans. I'm expected to get a babysitter for most things."

Elaine waved her away. "My pleasure. And it would be my pleasure to be a babysitter, too. But truthfully, I needed to get out of the house. If I refresh the listing one more time, I think I'll lose my mind."

Her spare rooms had been listed on a vacation rental app for over a week, but there hadn't been much traffic.

Charlene winced. "Still no hits?"

"A few 'hearts.' Whatever that means."

"Annette said that means people are saving your property for later! And apparently, it boosts your position in the search results."

Charlene shrugged. "There was something about an algorithm—I don't really know. But I hearted it!"

"So, two of the four hearts are yours and mine." Elaine bit back a sigh. Annette was almost certainly the third.

"Yeah, but *someone* out there saved it for later. And I bet more people will, too."

Elaine nodded. "Yeah, I suppose so. Maybe it will be useful eventually. But the hearts don't help me much now."

This whole time, she'd thought the only barrier to renting her extra rooms out was her own hesitance, but turned out, there was another factor she hadn't considered: renters.

What if no one wanted to rent from her?

The pictures Annette had taken looked great in the listing. At least, Elaine thought so. And the blurb they'd collaborated on was fun and inviting. But maybe her house wasn't nice enough. She didn't exactly have an ocean view, despite the name of one of the bedrooms. And a communal bathroom probably wasn't a huge draw for most people.

If renters were willing to walk, she had beach access. But beyond that, most people were likely looking for something more commercial. With mints on the pillows and a breakfast buffet spread every morning.

"I'm starting to think I should take it down," Elaine blurted.

"Take what down?"

"The house," Elaine said. "From the site. I think I should remove the rental."

"What? No! You can't."

Elaine's shoulders sagged. "I know you and Annette went to so much trouble for me. I'd feel terr—well, I *do* feel terrible. Because no one else seems to be appreciating it. I know how hard you both worked and what a good job you did, and I know taking it down would seem like you did all that work for nothing… but I don't know. I'm starting to feel like this whole thing was a mistake."

Charlene frowned. "Why would it be a mistake?"

"Because part of me isn't sure I want anyone to rent out the room. I mean, I want the money. *Need* the money, really. But the longer it goes without getting any interest, I can't decide if I'm more embarrassed or relieved. Ya know? Inviting someone into my house is scary."

"You're not wrong. I'm sure it's nerve-wracking," Charlene said evenly.

"And what if I don't even make any money? What if I go to all this work and stress and then this doesn't even solve my problem? I'm in the hole most months as it is, so it's possible renting out a room to a stranger helps me break even. *Maybe.*"

Charlene shrugged. "That's a possibility."

Elaine narrowed her eyes. "I thought you were going to try to encourage me. Maybe tell me I'm crazy."

Charlene leveled a serious look across the table. "Elaine, you are a lot of things, but you aren't crazy. In fact, you're completely right. This whole idea could crash and burn."

"Gee, thanks," Elaine chuckled.

"But you know what?"

Elaine almost didn't want to ask. "What?"

"If it does crash and burn, I won't feel for a second like I've wasted my time. In my opinion, you're always worth betting on."

Elaine smiled back. She was touched, really. She just wasn't sure what she'd done to deserve such high praise. After all, four hearts didn't exactly speak to wild success.

"I don't want syrup," Tyler interrupted, frowning at his pancakes. "And I want a big pancake, not little ones."

"But I already cut them up, Buddy," Charlene said.

"Put them back together. I want a big one."

Charlene glanced up at Elaine, fighting an eyeroll. "Welcome to my life."

Tyler was verging on inconsolable when Elaine's phone buzzed. The notification was from the vacation rental app. The first one she'd received since the fourth heart had appeared three days earlier. Elaine's heart launched into her throat as she clicked through to the message.

FINN S. has requested room 2A-MODEL CARS **for** TWENTY-EIGHT **days.**

Elaine gasped. "It happened. Goodness gracious, it really happened."

Tyler stopped arguing and turned to her. He and Charlene responded at the same time. "What happened?"

Elaine held up her phone. "A booking. Someone made a reservation. For one month."

"That's amazing!" Charlene clapped. "An entire month! That's a big deal. Congratulations!"

Elaine smiled, but she was running through the numbers in her head. One entire month. That was almost longer than she'd had the bed and breakfast idea. One month. One-twelfth of a year.

She was going to be living with a stranger for an entire month.

Elaine looked at the name again. "'Finn S.' is the name. It says he filled out the questionnaire and left me a message."

"I knew you were worth betting on." Charlene nudged Elaine's leg under the table. "Are you going to read what he said?"

Her finger hovered over the inbox icon, but before she could press it, Elaine clicked her phone off. "I'll check it later. We're eating right now."

"I don't mind if you want to check it," Charlene said. "This is amazing news."

"No, it's fine. I'll wait." Elaine's stomach was in knots.

Charlene shrugged. "Okay. But if you need help with anything, cleaning or stocking the room or whatever, you name it. I'd love to help."

"Thanks. If I think of anything, I'll let you know."

Like maybe trading houses. You come live in mine for a month; I'll live in yours. The prospect of fighting with a toddler about how to cut pancakes seemed more appealing than living with a stranger. A strange *man*, no less.

"Please do," Charlene insisted. "Your first guest. I can't believe it!"

Elaine did her best to look excited, but she couldn't believe it, either. She wasn't sure she wanted to.

That Afternoon At Elaine's House

Elaine stood in the doorway of the model car room and took a deep breath.

It had stopped smelling like kit glue and Old Spice ages ago, but the sharp smell of lemon cleaning products nearly wiped away even the memory of John. And while it was nice to see the model cars still on the walls of the rental unit, it was strange to see her past and future mashed together in such a visible way.

Elaine could remember when John built most of the model cars. The British sports car phase he went through right after they got married, banging out three in one week. Then he moved through the Corvettes and Camaros. The Volkswagen Beetle set was purely for Elaine.

"These silly little cars are going to look ridiculous when I get my shelves up," he'd said. At the time, all of his models were being stored in their kit boxes on the floor. "They'll stick out like sore thumbs."

"I think they'll look cute," Elaine had said. "Even cuter when they match the Beetle I'll have in the driveway."

He'd barked out a laugh. "Over my dead body."

The memory prickled now. John *was* dead. Elaine wasn't callous enough to go out and buy a Beetle, even though part of her thought John might appreciate the dark humor.

Each car represented a phase of their life, a season they navigated together. He built the 1977 Pontiac Trans Am when his dad died because *Smokey and the Bandit* was their favorite movie to watch together.

He started the Ford models when they were trying to have kids. By the time they began to lose hope, he'd finished models A, B, C, F, K, N, R, and S. The first car he finished after they installed his shelves was the Ford Model T.

Now, a stranger was going to walk into all that history.

"I'm not sure about this," she mumbled under her breath. "This was your private space. It's... sacred."

She could practically hear John laughing at her. *Sacred? They're cars, honey. Little bits of plastic, paint, and glue. Sell them all if the money would help. Or just chuck 'em all in the garbage if you need some shelf space.*

She'd never do that, of course. Because no matter what John said (or what she imagined he'd say), these models meant a lot to him. As long as she was alive, she'd keep them together.

But the fact remained that John would want her to be happy—not to mention financially secure. He'd hate that she was thinking about keeping the room as some monument to him rather than using it to pay the bills.

All of that in her head, perfectly logical and reasonable, still didn't make it easier to throw the doors open for the mysterious Finn.

If she was uneasy about letting Finn rent the room, then she shouldn't do it. Mason had had a point: Elaine was a woman alone. If Finn was dangerous or crazy, she'd have to fend him off on her own. She couldn't count on Mason stopping by randomly to check on her. It could be too late by that point.

What kind of person rented a room for an entire month, anyway? Maybe it was a trick. Maybe he was a vacation rental serial killer. He rented rooms for inordinately long amounts of time, murdered the host on day one, and then used the next twenty-seven days to destroy evidence and flee.

Elaine's heart raced. What kind of danger was she about to open herself up to?

There was still time for her to refuse his reservation and cancel the whole thing. Maybe that would be for the best. Yes, that's what she ought to do.

She pulled out her phone and opened the app. She clicked on Finn's name and once again saw his request to rent the Model Cars room for twenty-eight days. Just as she was working up the gumption to hit "Decline," she saw the red dot flickering in the top corner of the screen.

Finn's message.

It wouldn't be right to decline him without giving him a fair shake. She opened the message.

Hi there! I'm Finn Stratford, your potential renter. The questionnaire provided by the website didn't give me space to fully explain myself, so I thought I'd message you.

First of all, I'm a travel writer. I have a weekly advice column with Travel Insider *where I share travel and vacation tips, but I've also had two travel books published (I'll send along links to my work if you'd like to see the kind of content I write). I say all this not to brag, but instead, to beg you to accept my offer. I'm working on a series of* Livin' the Local Lifestyle *travel guides with the goal of helping people experience common travel destinations as the locals do.*

Second of all, your rental was one of the few I came across that wasn't trying to sell me a resort experience. I have no interest in infinity pools and booze cruises. I want to see what Isle of Palms is like for the locals, and your rental would be a great home base while I do my research.

Feel free to ask me any other questions you may have. I hope to speak with you soon.

Best,

Finn Stratford

P.S.: I attached screenshots of your photos with the cat circled in each one. I don't need twenty-five dollars off the cost of the room. I'm happy to pay full price. I just can't resist a challenge.

Elaine stared at the screen and then groaned aloud. "Darn it."

Finn Stratford was charming. And he had an interesting job with a valid reason for being on the island.

Still, letting someone come into her house while she was living there alone—

Her phone buzzed in her hand. The animal part of her brain panicked, worried she'd somehow hit something on the screen and video-called Finn. But it was just Annette calling.

"Hey, Annette."

"Hey, roomie!" Annette paused for a few seconds. "Assuming the offer still stands, of course."

Elaine was so surprised, it took her a second to wrap her head around what Annette was saying. "You're moving in?"

"It makes sense," Annette said. "I'd be close to Charlene and Tyler and I like the neighborhood. Plus, you need a renter and I need a room. We are kind of a match made in heaven."

Elaine chuckled. "Are you sure? I hope you're not doing this because you feel bad for me. Goodness knows you've already done me plenty of 'favors.'"

"*Me* feel bad for *you*? Are you forgetting I'm the unwed mother without a place to live? I don't have the energy to feel bad for anyone else. I'm too busy feeling bad for myself." Annette laughed. "But I promise to keep my pity party quiet so I don't disturb you or the other renters. No sad music on after 9 PM."

"Is the Ocean View room okay? The Model Car room was rented out earlier this afternoon."

Annette gasped. "You already rented out the other room? That's amazing!"

Apparently, she had. Elaine hadn't actually accepted Finn's request, but... well, now she couldn't think of a reason to refuse. He didn't seem to be a serial killer, she needed the money, and she wouldn't be alone in the house. She'd have a semi-permanent renter in Annette.

She looked around the room again, at the model cars shining in the low afternoon light. Her mind was far from clear, but she could practically hear John's voice when she said, "Yeah, amazing."

8

A FEW DAYS LATER—MORNING AT THE BEACH

Elaine stepped off the beach path. The damp sand sucked at her sandals and cordgrass tickled her ankles with every step. She usually stuck pretty close to the marked trail, but she'd seen Charlene and Tyler dart up the beach and disappear between the dunes. Her interest was piqued.

"What are you two doing back here?" Elaine asked when she rounded the bend and saw them hunched near the foot of a dune.

Charlene waved. "Tyler thought he saw a turtle hatchling."

"A loggerhead sea turtle," Tyler specified without looking up from the sand.

"Yes, sorry," Charlene said with a laugh. "A loggerhead sea turtle hatchling. He thought he saw it crawl through the grass."

Elaine looked around. "Are you sure? The little guy would be heading the wrong way."

"I need to take him to the water," Tyler said. "He has to live in the water. He won't surf... sur—"

"Survive," Charlene offered.

"He won't survive on land!"

He also might not survive in the ocean, but Elaine didn't want to be the one to deal that blow. Tyler would learn the difficult truths about the circle of life from someone else.

"Well, let me help in the search, then."

"You don't have to, Elaine. Really."

"Helping is just what friends do, right?"

Tyler nodded vigorously. "Right!"

Fifteen minutes later, Elaine had two ant bites on her ankles, half a dozen sandspurs stuck in her knees, and zero turtles of any variety.

"If there was a hatchling, I'm sure he found a safe place to hide," Charlene said.

Tyler pouted. "What if he got stuck?"

Charlene patted his head. "He'll find his way to the ocean. Don't you worry."

Tyler looked worried, but thankfully, he gave up the search once Charlene mentioned pancakes at home. They all trudged back towards the path.

"Sorry you got sucked into this."

"It's okay," Elaine said. "This was a better workout than my usual walk, anyway."

"Well, between you and me," Charlene whispered, "I don't think this was about the turtle. I think this whole turtle search has to do with Annette leaving."

Tyler was just out of earshot. He was walking ahead of them and kicking at the sand, sending it up in the air in puffs.

"Because she's moving?"

Charlene nodded. "Tyler has abandonment issues. As you can imagine."

Elaine actually felt her heart break a little. "Oh. I didn't even think— Poor kiddo."

"He'll be fine. I just might have to rehome a few wild animals until he adjusts," Charlene said. "We've told him that she is just moving in with you and will be right down the road."

"My house is your house. Y'all can visit anytime you want."

"Annette told him that, too. I just think he might need to see it to believe it, you know?"

"That makes sense," Elaine said. "Maybe once she is moved in, we can have y'all both over for dinner or something. That way, he can see where she'll be living."

"That would be great," Charlene said. "And actually, we're having a goodbye dinner at our house tonight. Maybe you could come along and offer some reassurance that way, too. It might make him feel better to have you there."

"Absolutely. I'll be there," Elaine said.

"Are you sure? I know tomorrow is a big day, what with Annette moving in and—wait, Finn is checking in tomorrow, too, right?" she asked. "If you're too busy getting ready for him, then don't worry about it. Tyler will be fine."

Elaine's stomach twisted at the mention of Finn. But she pushed the nervous feeling down.

"I'm quite sure. I'm all ready for the renters," Elaine lied. "What time is dinner?"

"How about seven?"

Elaine smiled. "See you at seven."

Dinner was a disaster.

"Why are we saying goodbye if she isn't leaving?" Tyler's eyes were red and puffy. Tears and snot ran down his face.

Charlene smoothed his hair back. "She's leaving our house, but she isn't—"

Tyler threw his head back and wailed. "She won't have a house?"

"Oh, Lordy," Annette groaned.

The dinner had started well enough. Tyler was playing with magnetic tiles on the floor when Elaine arrived. Charlene and Annette were in the kitchen.

"I made a white chocolate cake with white chocolate ganache and raspberry filling!" Annette had announced, spinning the cake on the cake stand.

"Is this what I have to look forward to when you live with me?" Elaine had asked. "Delicious baked goods all the time? I'm not sure my hips can handle it."

Charlene snickered. "The real question is whether your kitchen can handle it. Good luck and godspeed. Invest in sponges."

"I'm not that bad," Annette had given Elaine a nervous smile. "I'll clean up after myself. Don't worry."

Dinner was a roasted chicken with herbs in a butter sauce and white cheddar and thyme mashed potatoes. Apparently, Gregory had cooked the food and then dropped it off for them after the pot roast Annette left in the crock pot overnight inexplicably dried out.

"The crock pot is broken. It's the only rational explanation," Annette protested. "It short circuited and burned the food or... something. I don't know, but it wasn't my fault."

"Nothing ever is," Charlene had teased.

They ate and enjoyed each other's company and it all felt... relaxed. Normal. Elaine could almost picture these kinds of family dinners becoming a regular thing. They could take turns hosting every other week or twice a month. Elaine could cook, Annette could bake. It would be nice.

Then...

Charlene had stood up and raised a glass. "Annette, this last year living with you has been... Well, it has been a treat. You came back into my life right when I needed you most. You make the best cakes, give the best advice, and always know how to kick me in the rear when I need it. Metaphorically speaking."

"And literally, as needed," Annette had added. She was laughing, but her voice was thick with unshed tears.

"And literally," Charlene agreed. "Annette, Auntie Net... we are going to miss seeing you every day, but we—"

"What?" Tyler looked around, wide eyes blinking. "We won't see her every day?"

"Well, not *every* day," Charlene had said gently. "She'll be living in another house, so some days—"

And then chaos ensued.

Elaine had thought, for a bit, that Charlene was worried about nothing. Tyler had seemed okay with everything, like he was going to adjust fine.

But now, he was inconsolable, even with Charlene and Annette both tending to him. Elaine felt useless.

"She is going to have a house," Charlene was explaining. "Aunt Net is going to live with Miss Elaine. You know where Miss Elaine lives. We walk past her house all the time."

His eyes widened. "It's far away. Too far to walk!"

"We walk there all the—"

"What if I get sick and can't walk?" he asked. "What if I get sick and die?"

Annette laughed humorlessly. "Well, now we are way off topic. That's a whole 'nother thing to be sad about."

"Will Aunt Net come see me if I die?"

"If you're dead, then I won't be able to—"

Charlene elbowed Annette in the side. "Not the time, Aunt Net."

"Oh, right," Annette said quickly. "Yes, bud. I'll always come see you. No matter where you are. And no matter where I am."

He sniffled. "Always? Even when it's dark?"

"Even when it's dark," Annette assured him. "But in the middle of the night, I'll be sleeping, so I probably won't—"

She couldn't even finish before he started crying again. "You won't come see me in the middle of the night?"

Charlene groaned. "Tyler, *you* are sleeping in the middle of the night. You won't know if anyone comes to see you."

"I don't ever want to sleep!"

Charlene dropped her head in her hands in defeat. Annette stood back, looking dazed.

And Elaine watched it all helplessly from the far end of the table, her chicken going cold in front of her.

She should try to do something. Try to say something that would help. That's why Charlene had asked her to come to dinner, anyway, right? To make Tyler feel better?

Elaine cleared her throat. "Um, Tyler? I know you—I know this is a hard thing to understand. But Annette—Aunt Net isn't leaving forever. She isn't really even leaving."

He was still crying, but the volume seemed to turn down slightly. Elaine spoke up and continued.

"Aunt Net is still going to be close by and come see you a lot, but her bed is going to be in another house. In my house, actually." She cleared her throat. It felt less like talking to a four-year-old and more like trying to diffuse a bomb. "Aunt Net is going to live in my house, and you can come over anytime you want."

Tyler blinked and swiped his stuffed turtle toy across his nose. "I can come to your house?"

Charlene and Annette looked at each other. Elaine recognized the hope in their eyes. They looked like people lost in a desert who'd just spotted water.

"You can go see Aunt Net at Miss Elaine's house any time you want," Charlene said quickly.

"Anytime at all," Annette added.

Elaine nodded. "I'll even give your mom a key so you two can come and go whenever you want."

Remarkably, Tyler actually smiled. "You will?"

"Absolutely."

"I can come live with Aunt Net?"

Elaine's shoulders dropped. *Oh no.*

"Oh… well, um—" She sucked in a breath and held it, afraid what would happen if she said the truth.

Tyler looked around, waiting for an answer. "Can I live with Aunt Net?"

No one else seemed to want to answer, either. And Elaine had gotten them this far. Maybe if she was careful…

"You can visit," Elaine said with a smile.

Tyler turned back to her. "For forever?"

"Well…"

His lower lip quivered. Charlene hurriedly knelt down in front of him. "You are going to live here with me. In your room. With all of your stuffies. And your turtle. Who would feed and water Real Sheldon if you left?"

Tyler squeezed Stuffed Sheldon tightly against his chest. "Real Sheldon could come, too. We can all live with Aunt Net. Like we all live together now. Forever."

"Buddy," Annette said, "Miss Elaine's house isn't big enough for all of us. And this house isn't big enough for—"

Tyler turned to Elaine and shrieked. His eyes were narrowed, his teeth bared. It would almost be funny to see his sweet little face all twisted up if it wasn't so heartbreaking. He was hurting.

"I hate Elaine!" he screamed. "You are so, so… you are stupid! The stupidest!"

"Hey!" Charlene warned. "Tyler, that isn't—"

Elaine stood up. "It's okay. He feels like this is my fault, and—"

"It's *all* your fault," Tyler said, confirming her suspicions.

"Buddy, it isn't Miss Elaine's fault," Annette said. "She is letting me—"

Tyler threw his arms around Annette's neck. Over her shoulder, he stuck his tongue out at Elaine.

He was four years old. His emotions were always behind the steering wheel. Logic wasn't invited on the ride.

Elaine couldn't be angry with him. But that didn't mean it didn't hurt.

"I'm sorry," Charlene said. "He just... This is hard and he—"

Elaine waved her apology away. "I understand. Maybe I should just go?"

"No," Annette said. "You can stay, Elaine."

"No, she can't." Tyler frowned. "She can't stay here. Aunt Net can stay here. Not her."

"I'll go." Elaine backed away from the table. "Thanks for dinner. And I'll... I'll talk to you later."

And out she went. The night outside felt much colder than it had on the way here.

When she walked through the front door of her own house, she could hear the air conditioner humming. The ice maker in the freezer was dumping a new batch of ice into the tray.

It was the white noise of Elaine's life, routine and lifeless.

She'd been nervous all week about opening her home up to Finn and Annette, about inviting them into her space. But she knew it was time. If things were ever going to change, she needed to open herself up.

Or at least give it one heck of a try.

9

THE NEXT MORNING AT ELAINE'S HOUSE

Finn knocked on Elaine's front door at 9 AM sharp. For some reason, she was surprised.

Nine was the time they'd agreed to, but even though Elaine had sent his rental confirmation email, Finn had responded to it, and he'd paid his deposit, part of Elaine still didn't believe this was really happening. Somewhere deep down, she'd expected the day to come and go like any other—simple and quiet and empty.

But when she looked through the peep hole, there he was. On her front porch.

"Oh," she breathed. The only thing more surprising than Finn standing on her porch was how handsome he looked doing it.

Well, "handsome" might be a bit of a stretch, though not due to any fault of his own. Through the peephole, he was misshapen, stretched and morphed in the fish-eye lens. But Elaine could make out thick, dark hair, a trim frame, and an easy smile.

She jerked away from the door, worried for a second that he could tell she was gawking at him.

"Relax," she said quietly. "Be professional."

A few different articles online had suggested acting like you were a hotel manager. *The guest is not walking into* your *house. They are arriving for a stay in a room in a hotel—a place you have no real attachment to. What are they doing in their room? None of your business.*

"None of my business," she muttered. "Act like you've done this before."

Elaine took a deep breath and opened the door.

Finn was still smiling, and without the funhouse mirror effect from the peephole, he did in fact live up to the handsome billing. His dark hair was tousled by the morning breeze, with just a smattering of salt and pepper throughout, and a little dimple appeared on the right side of his face when he grinned. He was in his late fifties by the look of him, if she had to guess.

"Hi!" He stuck out his hand and then pulled it back. "This probably isn't a handshake situation."

He seemed nervous, which actually made Elaine feel better. "We don't have to be that formal," she said with a smile. "You'll be living here, after all."

"Home sweet home." He stepped back and admired the porch. "Deep porches aren't just from country music songs, are they? This is a proper porch. Look, you even have rocking chairs."

"Perfect for sweet tea and warm summer evenings," Elaine said. His excitement was endearing, if a little surprising. "Have you never been to the South before?"

"My beat is mostly in the Northeast, so I tend to stick up that way. I did go to a barbeque restaurant in Virginia once. Why, is my Yankee showing?"

Elaine shrugged. "Maybe a little. I'm just surprised. Your letter said you were a travel writer?"

"You read my letter?"

"I did. And I guess I should confirm… Finn, right?"

"Right," he nodded. "And Elaine?"

"Right."

He smiled. "I have to admit, Elaine, I didn't think you'd read my letter. I mostly wrote it out of desperation. I really wanted to stay here."

"Why? Well, I mean… Not to say my house isn't nice, but—" Elaine chuckled. "I think my house is wonderful, but there are a lot of rentals on the island. I'm sure you had plenty to choose from."

"Yeah, but I was hoping to stay in an actual house. A lot of the rentals were for empty units or guest houses. But I wanted a host who would be there to point me in the right direction. A tour guide. A… a Yoda to my Luke, if you will."

"Does that make me Yoda?"

Finn looked startled for a moment. "Only in the sense that you know more about the area than I do. You're wise."

"Not green and wrinkly, then? Good to know."

Finn smiled. "Not at all."

Be professional. Be a hotel manager.

"Forgive me, darling—we don't have to talk on the porch. Come on in." Elaine stepped aside as Finn rolled his suitcase through the door.

This was really happening. A strange man was in her house, suitcase in hand. And he wouldn't be leaving for quite some time.

Regrets and nerves swirled inside of her, but Elaine didn't give them a chance to settle. She just charged ahead.

"I can give you a quick tour if you want to follow me."

She pointed out the living room off to the right, the kitchen and dining room at the back of the house, and the half bath tucked beneath the stairs.

"Upstairs are the bedrooms. I've taped up laminated labels next to each room so you'll know which one is yours."

"The model car room," Finn nodded. "I used to love model car kits when I was a kid. I haven't built one in… gosh, ages. But I'm excited to check them out. Are they yours?"

"Yes. Or, no," Elaine corrected. It felt like she'd swallowed her tongue. "No, they aren't *mine*. Not exactly. I didn't build them, if that's what you meant."

Finn was still smiling, but his brow furrowed. Elaine sounded like a crazy person. She took a deep breath.

"My husband built them. My late husband. It was a hobby of his. I couldn't bear to take them all down off the shelves."

Enjoy your stay, Finn. Be sure not to trip on my emotional baggage on your way up the stairs.

Her face felt flushed. She was certain her cheeks were beet red.

He gave her a sympathetic smile. "I'm sorry to hear about your husband, but that's really nice—leaving the cars up. A little tribute."

"Yeah, sort of."

"And a selling point, too. They caught my eye!" If Finn was bothered by Elaine's oversharing, he didn't show it. He grabbed the handle of his suitcase. "I suppose I should make my way up, then. I don't want to bother you."

"You're not bothering me," she said. "I actually made a pot of coffee… if you like coffee. You're welcome to it."

He sighed. "I don't simply like coffee. I love it. I live on it."

Elaine laughed. "Well, okay, then."

"I'm not exactly a morning person. Pre-ten o'clock, I barely know which way is up."

Elaine pointed up the stairs. "Up is that way."

"You kid, but I'm serious." He smiled. "I'll get settled. But I'll be back for that cup of coffee."

"It will be ready for you."

Elaine watched Finn move up the stairs. As soon as he was out of sight, she hurried into the kitchen.

She was more nervous now than before she'd answered the door. But for a very different reason.

She'd lived alone for three years. Her conversation skills, especially with the male species, were rusty to say the very least. She knew how to talk to Charlene and Annette. But how should she talk to a stranger? How much should she reveal?

Elaine leaned onto the kitchen counter and dropped her face in her hands. She'd told him about her dead husband within five minutes of meeting him. Probably oversharing.

The ceiling above her squeaked and Elaine was instantly transported back. She could remember chopping vegetables in the kitchen for a chicken pot pie, Buddy Holly crooning through the Bluetooth speaker, and John padding around upstairs in his model room. Elaine always knew when he was coming downstairs because she'd hear the scrape of his chair across the floor, followed by the flick of him turning off his lamp.

But John wouldn't be coming downstairs.

"Get it together," she scolded herself.

Her first renter was going to be her last if she couldn't get a grip. *"Crazy woman talks to herself and imagines her dead husband is still in the house"* would be a very particular kind of rave review.

Elaine shook out her arms, stretched her back, and then set about being a hotel manager.

She pulled two coffee mugs out of the cabinet, grabbed the sugar canister out of the pantry, and slid both milk and cream into the center of the island. Eventually, she'd have to invest in a coffee bar. And a single-serve pot for the guests to use. But for now, this would do.

A few seconds later, she heard the telltale footsteps coming down the hallway and moving slowly down the stairs. Then Finn poked his head around the corner.

"Is this where I find the coffee?"

"It is." Elaine showcased the spread. "The pot is on the counter next to the fridge, but I have all the fixings here. I even have sweetener packets somewhere… but honestly, they've been in this house about as long as I have. You've been warned."

"Black coffee is fine with me." He poured himself a mug. "A little bit of cream, if I'm feeling indulgent. And after the night I had, I'm feeling indulgent."

"Uh-oh. Bad travel day?"

He shrugged. "Not the worst I've ever had, but not great. Let me tell you, that bed upstairs looked a lot more comfortable than the floor I slept on last night."

Elaine winced. "Ouch."

"Yeah, the Atlanta airport skimped on their carpeting. 'Threadbare' would be a generous description."

"Feel free to mention that when you write about your stay here."

"How does 'IOP: Beds More Comfortable Than the Floor' sound as a chapter heading?"

"It's a pretty low bar to jump over, but as a first review, I'll take it."

Finn frowned. "First review?"

"Well, yes. You're actually my first guest."

"Ever?"

Elaine sipped her coffee and nodded. "Ever. I only listed the house last week."

Finn looked around like he was seeing the place for the first time. Elaine didn't know if that was a good thing or not.

"Wow," he said finally. "Well, I'm honored."

She laughed. "Yes, it's quite an honor for you, staying in my guest room upstairs."

"It is, though. Isn't it?" He shrugged. "Letting someone into your house is a big deal. I meet a lot of people while I travel and I'm always touched when someone lets me into their orbit for a little bit. We only have so many days on Earth, so choosing to spend any of them with me is... well, it's not something I take for granted, I suppose."

Elaine felt a shiver move through her. She was a hotel manager at a front desk. This wasn't meant to get quite so personal.

Finn hadn't gotten that memo, it seemed.

"Sorry to make things all mushy," he laughed. "I guess I tend towards being a big sap most of the time. Maybe that's why I became a writer. Writers are supposed to be emotional."

"It was your letter that convinced me to go ahead with all this, actually," Elaine said, grabbing onto the change of conversation like a lifeline. "I was thinking about taking the listing down and cancelling the whole idea, but... oh, I don't know. Something about your letter caught my attention. I decided I'd give the whole rental thing a go."

Finn arched a brow. "Was it the way I begged? Or, no, it must have been my superior search and find skills. Did anyone else find the cat in every photo?"

"Like I said, you're the first," Elaine said. "So there's no one to compare you against. But I was still impressed. Ghost is a good hider."

"Ghost? Is that the cat's name?"

Elaine nodded. "Seems fitting, doesn't it?"

"I suppose I'll have to see the little guy and find out."

"He's already seen you." Elaine pointed over Finn's head at the refrigerator.

Finn turned around and jumped. He and Ghost were nose to nose. "Geez Louise!"

Ghost was perched on top of the refrigerator, his neck stretched out as far as possible to peer down at Finn. He looked like he was thinking about jumping on Finn's head.

"Okay. Ghost is a fitting name. Was he up there when I came down?"

"I have no idea," Elaine said. "He's sneaky."

"I'll say." Finn held out his hand and Ghost instantly rubbed his cheek into Finn's palm. "He's a friendly one."

"I think he likes you."

"I hope so," Finn said. "I love cats. That was another reason I wanted to stay here, actually. I travel so much that it isn't really feasible for me to have a pet."

"There's no one at home who could take care of a pet while you were away?" As soon as the question was out of her mouth, Elaine regretted it. "I'm sorry. I'm prying. I shouldn't—"

"Just me," Finn said. "That's why I want a pet. When I'm home, it gets quiet."

Elaine knew that feeling all too well, but she'd already done enough oversharing for the day. No need to spill all of her secrets to Finn.

"For as long as you're here, you can share mine," she said.

"You're a very generous host, Elaine." Finn scratched behind Ghost's ears and smiled over at her. She felt the warmth of it all the way down to her toes.

The Next Day At Elaine's House

Gregory and Annette walked into the kitchen and nearly collapsed into the bar stools.

"I did not sign up for this kind of physical labor," Gregory said.

Annette elbowed him. "Yes, you did. I said I could get movers, but you offered."

"Okay," he admitted. "I technically signed up for it, but… I'm not built for it. I'm a chef. I should be chopping things, not deadlifting dressers."

"Dramatic man." Annette patted his head and turned to Elaine. "We have been banging around for a while. I hope we aren't bugging your guest. What was his name?"

"Finn," Elaine said. "And he is out for the day, anyway. I sent him to Patriots Point to see the warship down there."

"The Yorktown?" Gregory asked.

"I think so. He is into that sort of thing—cars and planes and boats. He liked John's models upstairs, anyway, so I suggested it and he seemed keen."

Annette shot a curious look at Elaine, but Elaine ignored it. She knew what it meant and she wasn't anywhere near ready to talk about it. Finn was her guest. A guest in her hotel. She was being professional.

"That's for the best," Gregory said. "A mountain of Annette's clothes are currently blocking the hallway, so he wouldn't be able to get to his room."

"Not a mountain," Annette argued. "A small hill. I'm working on it, though."

Elaine waved her away. "Finn's life sounds pretty exciting. I'm sure he can scale a hill of clothes if necessary. Don't worry about it."

Gregory leaned in, voice low. "Between you and me, you might want to rethink letting her live here, Elaine. This is *before* she has a baby. Just think of the baby clothes situation if her own clothes are already—"

Annette tugged playfully on Gregory's red hair. "*Et tu,* Gregory? Traitor."

"What?" He shot her an innocent expression. "I was just telling Elaine how much fun the two of you are going to have here."

Annette pushed him towards the stairs. "Come help me with my clothes mountain, you liar."

Elaine chuckled as the two headed back upstairs for more unpacking. All morning, she'd been hearing their conversations and laughter floating down the stairs. The two of them hadn't known one another long, but they had a natural ease with each other.

She and John had been that way, too.

Elaine had always been shy, but John was bold. She'd been in the grocery store buying a gallon of milk, and John had just walked up to her.

"I'm sorry," he'd said, "but do you think you'd like to go out with me sometime?"

Elaine had looked around like maybe John was talking to someone else. The tall, thin man with the bright eyes and gentle smile couldn't have been talking to her. But he was.

"You," he'd confirmed, tipping his head towards her. "I know we don't know each other, but I'd like to know you. If you're interested."

She might be interested. But Elaine didn't date random men at the grocery store. She didn't speak with strangers. She didn't—

"Okay." That surprised him and her alike.

They'd left the store together, grabbed dinner at the Italian restaurant across the street, and that was that. They'd been inseparable.

Maybe it was loneliness and nostalgia turning her soft, but Elaine thought she saw the same rapport between Annette and Gregory.

Elaine was sitting on the back deck when Annette and Gregory came down again. She waved to them through the patio door when she noticed them looking for her.

"Wow. It's beautiful out here," Annette said when she stepped outside. She fingered the red trumpet vine. "I didn't realize you were a gardener."

Elaine shrugged. "I'm not, really. I just plant a few things at the start of the season, pluck weeds now and then."

Annette whistled. "I know where I'll be taking my morning coffee."

"You'll have to share the space with me," Elaine said. "I eat my breakfast out here most days."

"Sounds like we have a standing date, then." Annette squeezed Elaine's shoulder. "I'm officially moved in."

Gregory sighed. "We conquered Mt. Annette's Clothes."

"Get out of here." Annette bumped him gently with her hip. "I've had enough of your muscles and your teasing for one day."

"Do you want me to make you dinner?"

Annette shook her head. "Sorry, I can't. I have plans with Heather. We're going to a book signing in Mount Pleasant."

"Book signing for who?"

"I have no idea," Annette chuckled. "Some author she likes. But I haven't spent much time with her the last few weeks, so she called dibs."

Gregory pouted. "Can I tempt you to cancel?"

"Absolutely not. I made a promise. You're on your own tonight. I'll see you tomorrow."

"Fine." He pressed a kiss to her cheek. "Have fun. And Elaine, I'll see you around."

"I'm sure you will." Elaine had a feeling Gregory would be a regular visitor now that Annette lived with her.

"It's nice you're spending time with Heather," Elaine said once Gregory was gone. "She seemed really nice when I met her at that one dinner we all had."

"Yeah, she's great. A real character."

"Y'all must make a good pair, then. It's good to have friends."

"That's what they say," Annette chuckled.

"Instead of just a boyfriend, I mean." Elaine cleared her throat. "I wasn't great at that with John. When we got together I sort of... I gave him all of my attention. I lost a lot of my friends."

"Oh no."

"It wasn't a bad falling out. We didn't fight or anything," Elaine said. "We just stopped seeing each other as often. We grew apart. So it's good for you to prioritize staying in touch with them."

Annette nodded. "Charlene went through the same thing with Noah right at the start. I thought the two of them were going to merge into the same person there for a second. But she has it figured out now. And it's probably good for me to hear the reminder."

Elaine suddenly felt embarrassed. "I'm sorry. You didn't ask for my advice. I promise I won't make it a habit."

"I didn't ask, but that doesn't mean I don't appreciate it." Annette smiled. "Well, I better go get ready. I have to leave in an hour, so—"

"Go on then, dear," Elaine said. "Have fun."

When Annette was gone, Elaine turned back to her yard, the little square of grass and flowers she'd tended for over a decade now. What would her life look like if she'd tended all areas of her life so diligently? If she'd done even the tiniest bit of maintenance with her friends instead of shutting herself away with John for all those years?

Now that John was gone, Elaine couldn't bring herself to regret the time they'd spent together. She made the most of the time they had together and that's all anyone could ask for. Still, he was gone. And now she was alone.

It was time for her to figure out how to have friends again. How to build those relationships.

The trouble was, Elaine didn't even know where to begin.

10

A FEW DAYS LATER AT ELAINE'S HOUSE

"I swear, I've been late to work more the last week than ever." Annette sunk further into her deck chair and clutched her coffee. "It's just so beautiful out here."

"It's my favorite place," Elaine agreed.

It had been, anyway, back when things were normal. Especially in October when the weather cooled and the humidity ebbed. No matter what time of day you went outside, the temperature was perfect.

After they retired, Elaine and John would spend most of the morning out on the patio. Some days, they'd stay there and chat until lunch, long after their coffee had gone cold. Elaine had pictured it going on like that forever.

With no one to enjoy the view with the last few years, Elaine had enjoyed it less. But Annette was bringing some of the joy back.

Annette sighed. "But I should go. Apparently, watching the sunrise every morning for my mental health isn't a good enough reason to be late to work."

"Ridiculous."

"Right? And morning sickness that lasts all day isn't good enough, either."

"That is unjust," Elaine said. "But I made you that batch of lemon and ginger water we talked about yesterday. It's in the tall water bottle in the fridge. Grab it on your way out."

"Elaine, you angel." Annette squeezed Elaine's shoulder as she passed. "Thank you. I'll see you tonight for dinner?"

"I'll be here, darling."

It was amazing—Elaine wasn't leaving the house any more than she had been before, but the loneliness no longer consumed her. It was still there, like a lingering tickle in the back of her throat, but she could ignore it.

She had breakfast with Annette on the patio every morning. And they ate dinner together on the nights Annette didn't go to Gregory's. When that happened, and Elaine sat down at the table alone, Finn would often join her.

As was the case later that evening. "I had no idea you'd be feeding me so often," he said as he tucked into the country chicken and gravy. He wiped a bit of chicken gravy from his chin. "You're sure I'm not intruding?"

Elaine shook her head. "I like the company. Besides, I'd never finish the leftovers before they went bad. I haven't quite figured out how to cook for one yet."

Plus, she'd planned on cooking for a crowd tonight. Elaine thought maybe Annette and Gregory would both be joining her for dinner, but some "rock and roll gumbo group"—whatever that meant—was playing at The Windjammer, and Annette hadn't called to cancel until after Elaine had started cooking.

"Apparently, they're Gregory's favorite band," Annette had said apologetically.

Gregory's voice broke through the background. "They're a little rock and roll, a little jazz, a little country. A little of everything—like gumbo!"

Annette had chuckled. "Anyway, I'll be home late. Are you sure you don't mind me skipping out on you?"

"You live here now. Dinner isn't a date. You don't owe me anything."

Elaine really believed all of that, but she was still relieved when Finn had walked in. Before she had to figure out how to invite him to eat with her, he complimented the delicious smells coming from the kitchen.

"I'm glad I'm not bothering you because I don't think you could have kept me away," he said, talking around another bite. "Traveling as much as I do, I eat out a lot. A home-cooked meal is always welcome."

Elaine laughed. "Please don't tell me how my cooking compares to chefs around the country. I don't want to know."

"I mean, there's a time for eating a Michelin-starred chef's signature dish, but—"

"Is there? Because I've never found that time," Elaine joked.

"But," Finn continued, "nothing can compare to the love that goes in when you do it yourself. That's my opinion, anyway."

Elaine looked down at her plate. The breading on her chicken had gone a little soggier than normal. Fried chicken was one of John's favorites, but Elaine couldn't justify the in-depth process when she was just cooking for herself, so she was a little out of practice.

But the seasonings were still right on. White pepper tingled the back of her tongue, and the other spices—paprika, garlic powder, and ground ginger—worked so well together she almost didn't need the gravy. But John would never eat fried chicken without gravy.

"Sacrilege!" he'd say. "What am I supposed to dip my biscuit in if there's no gravy?"

Finn held up a piece of chicken, breaking her out of her reverie. "Seriously. Best fried chicken I can remember having in… a long time. Maybe ever."

"No need to flatter me. I won't evict you if you don't like it," Elaine teased.

Finn grinned and dug in for another bite. As much as she demurred, Elaine believed his compliments. He certainly backed it up with the way he ate. If he wasn't a grown man, she'd tease him about a growth spurt.

Though he was rather tall. Broad-shouldered, too. He had to eat something to maintain that kind of healthy girth.

Too many thoughts of Finn left Elaine flushed. She decided to look down at her own plate, too. "You made it to Patriots Point the other day, right? How was it?"

"The USS Yorktown! It definitely earned a mention in my book."

"A positive mention?"

"I try to keep all of my writing positive. It's more fun that way."

"How do you warn people away from the tourist traps?" Elaine asked.

Finn swirled his biscuit around the plate, mopping up the excess gravy. "I only talk about the places I recommend. I can tell people to make a stop at Superior National Forest in Minnesota without mentioning that their 'world's largest ball of twine' isn't actually the world's largest. I just leave it off the list."

"Minnesota lied about their ball of twine? Some people have no shame."

Finn shrugged. "That all depends on how you measure it. And where you live. Everyone wants to think their ball of twine is the biggest, don't they?"

Elaine raised a brow. "How else could you measure it? Either it's the biggest or it's not."

"Ah," he said, holding up a finger. "But some places measure by height, some by weight, some by width. It's a hotly contested topic. But last I heard, the largest ball of twine is actually in Kansas."

"Wow. How big?"

"I have no idea," he admitted. "But you won't catch me writing about it. I don't want to deal with the hate mail."

Elaine laughed. "You're kidding."

"I wish I was."

"You'd really get hate mail about twine?"

"You'd be surprised. People get passionate about that kind of thing. I get enraged emails if I get something wrong about a place I visit. Or if I leave off a beloved landmark that I didn't *belove* quite as much as I should have."

"I never would have guessed a travel writer would have to deal with that kind of thing."

"Occupational hazard," he said. "But Yorktown gets a positive mention. And today, I went on the Barrier Island Eco Tour you mentioned. It was great. Nothing negative to say, but I will have to warn people about the smell."

"What smell?"

"The tour guide called it something… I typed it up in my notes." He grabbed for his phone.

"Pluff mud?" Elaine asked.

Finn snapped. "That's it. The guide described it as 'layers of decay.' Not exactly picturesque, but I'm sure I can make it sound appealing."

"You could tell them that if you live here long enough, you hardly notice it," Elaine said. "But I do remember smelling it really strongly when we first moved here."

"We?" he asked. "You and your family?"

"Me and John," she said. "We moved here right after we got married."

Finn rested his chin on his fist, looking genuinely interested in her mundane life story. His life was so exciting that she highly doubted it.

"Where were you before?"

"Knoxville, Tennessee."

"Did you grow up there?"

"Close. I grew up in Oak Ridge. It's a small little town just outside—"

"I've been there!" he said. "It was one of the sites built to produce atomic weapons in the '40s."

Elaine was impressed. "You know your history."

"I wrote about the secret cities of the Manhattan Project years ago. I only know about history when I'm getting paid to know about it," he laughed. "It was a nice town, though. So is Knoxville. And Isle of Palms, from what I've seen."

"I've enjoyed them all. But I also haven't been many other places. I've suck pretty close to home for the most part. I probably wouldn't make a great travel writer."

"And I'd make a bad inn owner. We all have our things."

"It might be too soon to call this 'my thing.' You're my first guest."

"And a very satisfied one. Five stars," he declared, thumping his fist on the table. "For both the fried chicken and the company."

Elaine felt her cheeks flush. She'd give the company five stars, too, if anyone cared about her rating. It was better than talking to an old picture in a frame.

She glanced up at John. He was smiling down at them the way he always was. Elaine imagined the real John—*her John*—standing behind the portrait like in those old Scooby Doo cartoons, with the eyes cut out so he could peek through.

It was ridiculous. John would be happy she was talking to someone. Even a handsome travel writer. He'd be relieved she had people in the house again.

But Elaine knew better than to argue with her guilt. It didn't play fair. Never had.

Elaine picked up her dirty plate and carried it into the kitchen. "Well, if things go well the rest of this month, feel free to give me a mention in your book, too."

"You sure you're ready for that kind of fame? I have a small but mighty fanbase."

She smiled. "As if the model car rented room could really warrant a 'Sight to See' in your book."

"People like places with strong personality and charm." Finn shrugged. "The room has both of those things. So do you."

Elaine's heart pattered. She quickly turned on the faucet to scrub at her dish. She needed something to do with her hands.

Finn came up behind her with his tableware and set it neatly next to the sink. "But once it's published, everyone who comes here will expect a hot meal and good conversation. You might regret it."

Even the sound of the water couldn't drown out the thudding of her pulse.

She shook her head. "No," she said in a raspy croak. "I don't think I will."

11

THE NEXT DAY—MIDDAY AT ELAINE'S HOUSE

Tyler shined the flashlight on the baseboard across the room and waited. His shoulders crept closer to his ears with every second. The grin on his face spread. He looked like he was about to burst with anticipation.

And then…

A black fur ball darted out from under the armchair. Ghost swatted at the circle of light on the wall, sending Tyler into a fit of giggles.

"We shouldn't torment the cat," Annette said. "Are you sure you don't want to play with the train set? I'm having a great time."

Elaine had bought a few toys to keep at her house for when Tyler came to visit Annette. So far, she and Annette had connected a figure-eight track for the little train cars, but Tyler hadn't even glanced at them. Ghost was the star of the show.

"He likes it," Tyler said. "We're having fun."

He spun in a circle, trailing the light behind him. Ghost hopped after him. It was a clumsy kind of dance routine.

"It's fine," Elaine said. "Ghost naps most of the day away. The exercise is good for him."

Really, Elaine didn't know quite what Ghost did all day. Unless he was begging for food or looking for a cuddle, he made himself scarce. There was a reason they'd named him Ghost.

But either way, Elaine didn't mind. A little chaos wasn't such a bad thing.

Annette tossed a piece of train track back into the bucket and leaned against the couch. "Fine. I could use the break, anyway. Chasing Tyer around the beach this morning wore me out. I don't have as much energy as I used to."

"Creating a baby will do that to you."

"Apparently." Annette smiled and patted her stomach. "Worth it, though."

Elaine scooched in closer. "So, everything is going okay, then?"

She and Annette lived together now and Annette had the basic details, but they hadn't had a deep chat about the baby situation since Annette had first confided in Elaine that she was pregnant.

"Just a bit of morning sickness and fatigue. The usual stuff."

"Yeah, right." Elaine didn't want to pry, but… "And Frederick?"

Her ex-husband's name didn't exactly bring a smile to Annette's face, but she didn't look as put out as she could have. "The usual there, too. He's still being weirdly agreeable, letting me make all of the conditions for the divorce and custody. But I suspect he'll change his tune and start making some demands eventually. For now, it's all gravy."

"Well, that's good. Sometimes, these arrangements can be a real mess."

"Frederick is just trying to make things right. He feels guilty about *everything.*"

Annette waved her hand in the air, which struck Elaine as a remarkably casual way to encompass the way her husband had cheated on her for three years, had a baby with someone else, and then gotten Annette pregnant after he'd left "the other woman" and come crawling back.

"As he should," Elaine said. "He owes it to you to make things as easy as possible. You're going through a lot right now."

Tyler inched the flashlight across the living room floor. Ghost kept his green eyes trained on it, shoulders low and tail high in the air.

Then Tyler jerked the light up next to Annette. Half a second later, Ghost leapt through the air and slammed into the couch cushion, narrowly missing Annette's face. She yelped while Tyler squealed in delight.

"Only on the floor," Annette warned her nephew. She reached out to comfort Ghost, but he was already gone, darting across the room to catch the light now at Tyler's feet.

"Not my feet!" Tyler giggled, the light bouncing around as he tried to run away. Ghost pounced at it again and again.

"I'm sorry," she sighed.

"It's fine. Really."

"It's chaotic."

"Yeah. But a good kind of chaos."

Annette smiled. "That's true of a lot of things, isn't it? Raising a child alone is obviously a lot, but... I feel kind of grateful, too. To Frederick. Is that weird?"

"You're grateful?"

"Well, without Frederick, none of this would have happened—the good or the bad. I know the bad was *really* bad, but at the same time, the good has been really good. You know?" She shook her head. "I sound crazy."

"No," Elaine said. "No, you don't. I get it, I think. It's complicated, but you've always wanted a baby. Now, you have one. I suppose you could complain about the way you got it, but what's the point?"

"Exactly. I never imagined things would happen this way, but this is how they happened. This is the reality I've got. So I might as well make the best of it."

Suddenly, there was a crash from the other room. Elaine hadn't noticed Tyler and Ghost leave, but the living room was empty now.

"Oh no." Annette jumped up and ran out of the room.

Elaine probably should have been worried about the crash, but her mind was elsewhere—stuck on something Annette had said.

This is the reality I've got. So I might as well make the best of it.

Isn't that what Elaine had been telling herself whenever her guilt about John reared its ugly head? Of course, all else equal, she'd rather have John back. She'd rather share her meals with him and talk to him.

But he wasn't there anymore. Elaine was alone, and she couldn't sit around in a puddle of grief for the rest of her life.

She had to live.

Annette came around the corner holding the flashlight in one hand, squeezing Tyler's hand in her other. "TV time," she announced. "You're going to watch an episode of something and then we'll go scrounge up some lunch, kapeesh?"

"Got it." Tyler crawled onto the sofa and plopped down between them. His feet dangled over the edge of the sofa, bouncing with the energy still bottled up in his little frame.

Once he was set up watching some show about a cat who worked as a park ranger, Elaine and Annette moved into the kitchen.

"I know there are a lot of studies about how bad screen time is for kids, but I don't know how parents survived before television." Annette sagged into the bar stool at the island. "I need wine."

"I have apple juice," Elaine teased.

"Wonderful. I'll close my eyes and pretend it's sangria."

Elaine fetched it for her. Annette closed her eyes and took a sip. Then, with a deep breath, she opened her eyes and smiled. "So, let's talk about you now."

"Me? What about me?"

"I don't know," Annette shrugged. "How are... things?"

"Fine."

"How is the inn going? I haven't seen much of Finn around. Is he an easy tenant?"

"As easy as could be. He comes and goes. We had dinner together last night."

Annette raised one brow. Elaine knew that look far too well. Around Annette, Elaine sometimes felt like an unwed daughter in a Jane Austen novel, with Annette playing the role of matchmaker mother.

"He showed up right as I finished cooking. And I made too much because I thought you and Gregory were going to eat with me. It was professional," she said. "I was just doing my duty as a good host."

"You made us dinner?" Annette blinked guiltily.

"It was nothing."

"And I cancelled on you! I'm so sorry, Elaine. I had no idea you'd already—"

Elaine grabbed her friend by the shoulders. "It's fine. I have to eat, too. The food was for me. I would have made it with or without you and Gregory."

That wasn't entirely true. If it had just been her, Elaine probably would have baked some frozen chicken and made a batch of garlic rice. But regardless, what Annette didn't know couldn't hurt her.

"You're sure?"

"Positive," Elaine said. "Besides, the extras let me feed Finn, which he appreciated. He even joked about mentioning his stay here in the book. If he did, that could be a boost for business."

"What I'm hearing is that me bailing on you was actually the best thing to ever happen to you. Career-wise, anyway."

Elaine chuckled. "Exactly."

"And… on a personal level," Annette prodded, "are you and Finn… friendly?"

"Not in the way you mean it."

Annette frowned. "But *could* you be?"

"No. Well, I don't know. I don't even want to think about it."

She hadn't been able to sit and talk to Finn over dinner without feeling guilty about John. Letting herself think about anything beyond basic friendship might actually destroy her. It was safer to not even go there.

Annette pushed her juice aside and scooted closer to Elaine. "Is it because of John? Are you not ready, or… ?"

Elaine's instinct was to change the subject. But you can't keep your whole world bottled up and expect people to keep wanting to be a part of it.

This house had been closed up for long enough. It needed fresh air.

"I am ready," Elaine admitted. "Or at least, I want to be ready. I miss having someone to talk to about everything. Someone to depend on."

"And you deserve that!"

Elaine nodded. "I know. But I still don't think I'm ready. Because I really just want that person to be John. And no one else could ever be John."

"Oh, Elaine." Annette pulled her in for a hug. Her words were muffled in Elaine's hair. "I'm sorry."

She knew dumping her problems on Annette was a bad idea. Now Annette was pregnant and hormonal and worrying about her. "It's okay. I'm fine. Really."

"I know you're fine. But that doesn't mean you aren't hurting, too."

"Hm."

"What?" Annette asked.

"I guess you're right. I'm fine… really, since you and Finn showed up, I've been better than fine. It's been nice to have people in the house again. To have some company. But as nice as it is, it hasn't fixed everything."

"Of course not. No one thing will fix it all."

Elaine took a deep breath. And for the first time in a long time, it felt a little easier. To fill her lungs. To lift her shoulders. Like a burden had been plucked off.

"Thanks," she smiled at Annette. "But let's change the subject now."

Annette nodded. "Agreed. Something light. Cheery. How about—"

Before she could finish her thought, the front door thudded open. Elaine assumed it was Finn. He had a key, after all. But when the figure appeared in the doorway, teary-eyed and shaking, Elaine caught her breath.

"Charlene?" Annette jumped up and ran to her sister. "Are you okay?"

Charlene didn't say anything. She just shook her head.

"What is it?" Annette asked. "Is it Tyler? No. He's in the other room. What is it?"

Elaine stood up and pulled out a stool for Charlene. The woman accepted it silently, practically collapsing onto the seat. She swiped at her eyes and swallowed a lump in her throat.

"I just got a call—"

"From who?" Annette interrupted. "Was it about the adoption? Is Noah okay?"

Elaine laid a hand on Annette's arm. Annette stilled and nodded. "Sorry."

"I just got a call," Charlene repeated, "from Margaret."

If they'd been in a movie, Elaine and Annette would have gasped at the mention of Charlene's estranged daughter. Instead, they just stared at Charlene in silence, waiting for more pieces of the puzzle.

"Well, from the police, actually," Charlene corrected.

At that, Annette did gasp. "Is she okay?"

"She's alive," Charlene shrugged. "But she's been arrested. Again."

There was a weariness in her voice that Elaine had never heard before. Charlene didn't talk much about Margaret.

For years, Elaine had assumed Charlene's daughter was off living a wonderful life somewhere far away. Too far away to visit often, which would explain why Elaine hadn't seen her in years.

But then Margaret had dumped Tyler on Charlene's doorstep and the whole ugly truth had come out.

"Drugs?" Annette asked.

Charlene nodded. "What else? It's always drugs with her, isn't it? It always will be."

Elaine wanted to disagree. To offer up some hope. But everyone knew they'd be empty words. Whatever Margaret was into, she was in deep.

"I'm sorry, Char." It was all Elaine could think to say.

Charlene gave her a sad smile. "Me, too, Elaine. Me, too."

12

MIDDAY AT ELAINE'S HOUSE

Tyler's show ended before Charlene could explain herself.

"Do I gotta go home now?" Tyler asked as soon as he saw Charlene in the kitchen.

The normally decisive Charlene looked like a deer in the headlights. She blinked and opened her mouth, but nothing came out.

"I'd love to take Tyler on a walk, if you wouldn't mind," Elaine said. It was the only helpful thing she could think to do. Give Charlene a few minutes to talk to Annette and gather herself. "Maybe we could go—"

Tyler frowned. "What about Aunt Net?"

"What about me?" Annette asked, kneeling in front of the little boy.

"I'm 'sposta spend the day with you. That's what you said."

"We spent the morning together, though."

Tyler didn't look convinced. He crossed his arms and popped his lower lip out into a very potent pout. It tugged at Elaine's heartstrings.

"You can come see me anytime, buddy," Annette said. "But I need to talk to your mom, so maybe—"

"You said we were gonna eat lunch," he argued. "Kapeesh!"

"What?"

"Kapeesh!" he said again. "Lunch. Kapeesh."

Annette sighed. "I did promise you that, didn't I?"

He nodded. "Mhmm."

"And you're going to hold me to it, aren't you?"

Tyler offered up a tentative smile, sensing he'd won this battle.

Annette turned back to Charlene. "I'm sorry, Char. I promised him. Will you be okay to—"

"I'll be fine," Charlene said. "Y'all go along."

Tyler whisked Annette out the front door not even a second later, leaving Elaine and Charlene alone together.

After another second, Charlene stood up. "I guess I should get out of your hair. I'm sorry for showing up the way I did and—"

"You don't have to go."

"I should go," Charlene said again. "I got the call and knew Annette would be here. I overreacted."

"You didn't. You got a call from the police. Anyone would have reacted the same way."

Charlene tipped her head towards the front of the house. "I broke into your house."

"The door was unlocked," Elaine said. "Plus, this is your sister's house now, too. You're welcome here whenever you want, sweetheart. Just like Tyler."

Charlene sagged in her seat and pressed her forehead against the countertop. "I have no idea what to do."

"What did the police say exactly?"

"They just told me Margaret had been arrested. They didn't offer up a lot of other details."

"They told you it was drugs?"

"They didn't have to. I know." Charlene pursed her lips. "That isn't even what's bothering me. Not really. Because when I saw that it was the police department, I assumed it would be Margaret calling me. I assumed I would be her one phone call. But then, I answered and—" Charlene's voice cracked. "I answered, and it was an officer and… my first thought was that Margaret was—that she'd—"

She didn't need to finish the sentence. Elaine understood.

She squeezed Charlene's shoulder. "I'm sorry. That must have been horrible."

"I was so relieved," Charlene said. "I was relieved to find out my daughter had been arrested. Can you imagine? Because at least she was alive. But now… I have no idea what to do."

"Do you want to bail her out?" Elaine didn't have much in the way of money to offer, but if Charlene needed the help, she was sure she could scrape something together.

"That's just it: I don't know." She shrugged. "I've buried myself in taking care of Tyler and moving in with Noah. Without really meaning to, I'd shoved all these bad thoughts and worries about Margaret down so deep… and as soon as that phone rang, they shot right back up. And I don't think I can shove them down again."

"That's understandable. She's your daughter."

"Exactly. *She's my daughter.* I should be the one to help her out of this," Charlene said. "I should know what to do."

Elaine shook her head. "I don't have kids, but I'm pretty sure parents never know what to do. That's the general consensus, at least. You're just making it up as you go."

"I mean, do I bail her out?" Charlene asked. "If I let her sit in jail, am I a terrible mother?"

"You're not a terrible mother no matter what you decide."

"But will she think I am?" Charlene's brows were pinched together. She looked older than the last time Elaine had seen her, just a few days earlier. "And if Margaret thinks I'm a terrible mother, she might not come to me if she's really in trouble. And if I get a phone call in a few months or years that—that she's... dead... I wouldn't forgive myself."

"None of this is your fault, though," Elaine said. "Margaret has made her choices."

Charlene nodded, but Elaine didn't think she was really listening. "But then again, if I bail her out, she'll probably go right back to what she's been doing. And what if she overdoses? I'd blame myself for that, too. Because at least in jail, she's safe from her own horrible choices."

Elaine wrapped an arm around her shoulders. It was the only thing she could think to do. "I'm sorry. I wish I could help."

"Thanks," Charlene mumbled, her face in her hands once again. After a few seconds, she took a deep breath and sat up. "But this is my mess. Well, it's Margaret's mess... which makes it my mess."

"And you're my friend," Elaine said softly. "Your messes can be my messes, too."

When Charlene looked up again, her eyes were misty. But she didn't cry. Elaine could tell she was holding it back.

They walked together to the front door. Before she left, Charlene squeezed Elaine's hands. "You're a good friend, Elaine."

"I do my best, dear. Same as you."

That night in bed, Elaine pulled her comforter up around her chin, her conversation with Charlene rolling around in her head.

She'd already been in her room when Finn finally came home, and Annette had texted earlier in the evening that she was staying with Gregory. Maybe Elaine should have been worried about being in the house alone with a near-stranger sleeping one room over, but she found the sounds of Finn puttering around in his space comforting.

Sometimes, it was just nice to know someone was there.

Hopefully, she'd been that person for Charlene. Even though she couldn't help, maybe listening to her had been enough.

Charlene had said she was a good friend. Elaine wanted to prove her right. She wanted to help Charlene—and Margaret, by extension. But how?

Nothing came to mind. She fell asleep wondering, hoping for clearer answers in the morning.

13

MORNING AT HARRIS TEETER GROCERY STORE

Elaine had so many ideas.

Grab and go breakfast bags she could set out on the island.

A sandwich bar with a panini press.

And maybe she could invest in some of those silver dinner trays with lids. Future guests might not be as interested in eating with Elaine at the dining room table. Not like Finn. In which case, she could carry meals up to them.

She was probably getting ahead of herself.

"You're like a runaway horse sometimes," John used to tease. "When you get an idea, *bang*. You're off!"

"Then you best learn to hold on," she'd respond every time.

But in this case, she probably ought to just stick to the lists Finn and Annette gave her. It had been hard enough to get the lists from them in the first place.

"I can do my own shopping," Annette had argued. "You don't need to buy me anything."

Finn had outright refused. "Absolutely not. You've fed me four nights in the last week. You don't need to do anything else for me."

But after assuring them she'd let them pay her back for the groceries, they relented and gave her some things to scoop up.

Annette's requests were largely fueled by pregnancy cravings. A loaf of cheese and garlic bread, mango yogurt cups, cream soda.

But Finn's revealed exactly how he maintained such a trim physique. Half of Elaine's cart was fresh produce and leafy greens.

Matter of fact, she was actually doubling back to the produce department because she forgot Finn's cucumbers when she nearly T-boned someone. All it took was one look for Elaine to recognize Betty Claine standing in front of her.

"I'm sorry, excuse me," Betty said, struggling to unwedge her cart from the corner of the potato bin. She chuckled. "Darn thing has got me. I'm so sorry."

"Betty," Elaine said gently. "Hi there."

When Betty looked up, her eyes were blank. For one horrifying second, Elaine thought her old friend had forgotten her. They *were* old friends, after all. Or old coworkers, at least. Elaine hadn't seen Betty in ten years. Not since she'd retired.

Then, thankfully, Betty's face lit up. "Elaine!" Cart forgotten, she pulled Elaine in for a hug. "My God. How are you, honey? How have you been? It's been ages!"

"Ages and ages," Elaine agreed. "I'm fine. How are you?"

"Clumsy as ever," Betty laughed. Laugh lines Elaine didn't remember ringed Betty's mouth and crinkled her eyes. Otherwise, she looked the same. Pitch black hair streaked through with gray, her lips painted their customary bright red.

"I can't believe this is the first time I've run into you here."

"I usually make the trek to the Saigon market. Hot tip: don't buy sesame oil here," Betty whispered, holding up a large glass bottle. "It's three times the price it ought to be."

Asian cuisine was way outside Elaine's comfort zone in the kitchen, but she nodded anyway. "I'll remember that."

"I only came here because I'm in the middle of making lunch. Everyone is going to be at my house in two hours, and I ran out of at least three different ingredients I always have on hand." She shook her head. "Isn't that about how it goes, though?"

"It sure is." Elaine couldn't remember the last time she'd cooked for a large group of people, so she really couldn't say. "Who do you have coming over? Family?"

"My Zumba girls," she said, wiggling her hips a little. "I became an instructor after I left the clinic."

"You left? Like, retired?"

Elaine had just been promoted to office manager of the clinic when Betty was signed on as a therapist. Her office door was just across from Elaine's. For the five years they worked together, Betty was Elaine's closest work friend.

Betty shrugged. "I feel a little too young to run around telling people I'm retired, but I suppose I am. Peter is still working at the hospital, but I decided to quit and stay home. During the school year, I teach a few dance classes throughout the week. I like to get everyone together for a potluck once every month or two. It's hard to chat when you're dancing."

"Wow. How fun!" Dancing for exercise sounded like a torture sandwich, but she could tell Betty was excited about it.

"I think so," Betty smiled. "My kids are endlessly embarrassed by me, but when aren't they?"

"Kids? Last time I knew you only had—"

"That's right! We haven't talked since Jenny came along." Betty beamed. "She's nine now. Justin is fourteen."

Elaine could remember dark-haired little Justin running around her legs in the lobby on the rare times Betty had to bring him with her into the office. About the same age Tyler was now. Betty had seemed on the older end of motherhood at the time—forty with a four-year-old. And then to have another kid five years later? Elaine tried to imagine herself raising a teenager and a pre-teen and couldn't do it. No, thank you.

"Bless your heart, that's amazing," Elaine said. "It feels a little ridiculous to say congratulations after all this time, but... congratulations."

Betty laughed. "Thank you. And what about you? Any big life changes?"

John's name sat on the end of her tongue, but Elaine bit it back. She didn't want to be a downer. Not when Betty was telling Elaine all about her family and her friends and her hobbies. Ten years apart and all Elaine could think to say was that her husband had died?

"I just opened a bed and breakfast. Well, sort of," she said. "It's only a few rooms. But I have my first renters right now."

"Vacation rentals! That's a good business to be in living around here. Peter and I have considered it, but it seems like more work than we're willing to put in."

"It's only my first month, so I can neither confirm or deny." Elaine smiled. So far, it all felt manageable. But she also wasn't raising children and leading dance lessons.

Betty checked her watch and jolted slightly. "Shoot. I really have to go."

"Oh, of course, darling," Elaine waved her on. "Go ahead. Sorry to hold you up."

"You didn't. Well, actually, you did," Betty laughed. "But it was nice. I was glad to be held up."

"Me too. It was nice to see you."

When she'd left the clinic, Elaine remembered promising Betty they'd still see each other. *"I have your cell number. I'll call you and we'll go out for lunch or something,"* Elaine had said. *"You can give me all the drama around here now that I'll be out of the loop."*

Betty had squeezed her in a hug. *"You promise?"*

After Elaine left, she never called. Not once. She wondered if Betty remembered that conversation.

Probably not. It seemed like Betty had more than enough to keep herself busy. Her life was full, vibrant. Honestly, it was hard to ignore the pinch of jealousy in Elaine's gut. Even though she was happy for her old friend, she couldn't help but wish she had as many bright, shiny life updates to share.

Betty was walking away when Elaine called after her. "Hey, Betty?"

She spun around. "Yeah?"

"I know you're in a hurry, but maybe some other time, if you're free, we could—we could meet up again. Like this." Elaine shook her head. "Well, not like this. Maybe we could meet up on purpose. Like, for—"

"For lunch?" Betty asked, her mouth tilting up in a smirk. "You're ten years late on that promise."

Elaine felt her cheeks warm. "Oh. Sorry about that."

Betty shrugged. "Better late than never. How about tomorrow?"

The Next Day At Front Beachtro

Elaine nearly dropped with relief when she walked into Front Beachtro and saw Gregory waiting tables. She needed a familiar face today.

He waved as soon as she walked in. "Sit anywhere, Elaine. I'll be with you in a minute."

She chose a table in the middle of the dining room. Not too close to the kitchen where they'd hear the kitchen staff or too close to the door where they'd get a draft. It was Elaine's favorite spot. Hopefully, Betty wouldn't mind it.

Elaine looked through the front window. The sidewalk was clear. They hadn't said whether they'd meet out front or inside, so Elaine had to keep watch and make sure Betty wasn't standing outside waiting for her.

This whole lunch date had been a complete whim. A fine enough decision in the moment, but after a night and morning spent stewing, Elaine was suddenly nervous. What if she and Betty didn't have anything to talk about? Ten years was a long time. Maybe they wouldn't get along as well as they used to.

"Are you ready to order?"

Elaine was so busy panicking, she hadn't noticed Gregory walk over.

"Hey!" she jumped. "No, actually. Well, I'll take a water. For now. I'm waiting for someone."

Gregory's brows shot up. "Anyone I know?"

His smile made it obvious he hoped it was Annette. If Elaine didn't adore both Gregory and Annette, their puppy love would make her roll her eyes.

"I doubt it," she said. "Just an old friend I'm meeting up with. Her name is Betty."

"Dark hair and red lipstick?"

Elaine frowned. "Do you know her?"

Gregory pointed out the front window. "No, but I think I see her out the front window."

Sure enough, Elaine looked over and Betty was standing on the sidewalk, looking up and down the street.

"Oh no! I knew I should have waited outside. I'll go—"

"No, I'll go," Gregory said. "Don't get up."

Elaine wanted to argue, but Gregory was already gone. She watched him open the front door and call to Betty. Any apprehension she had about a strange man calling her name was wiped away by Gregory's easy charm. He grinned and held the door open for her.

"Is this your first time with us?" Gregory asked Betty as they walked towards the table.

She nodded. "It is. I've heard good things, but haven't been in yet. You just opened, right?"

"A couple months ago," Gregory confirmed. "If you have any questions, let me know. Though, your friend is one of my best regulars. I'm sure she can answer any questions you have as well as I can."

When they reached the table, Gregory pulled out Betty's seat. She looked flushed. Happily married as she was, it was hard not to be smitten with the likes of Gregory Dane.

"I'll be back with some water and tea for you lovely ladies?" Gregory asked, looking from Elaine to Betty to confirm.

"Yes, please," Elaine said. "Thanks, Gregory."

Gregory winked at her and hurried back to the kitchen. As soon as he was gone, Betty chuckled. "I had no idea I'd be getting the royal treatment here. You're a good friend of the owner, apparently?"

"Kind of," Elaine said. "I'm friends with his girlfriend. She's actually renting out one of my spare rooms."

"Girlfriend. That makes sense. A man like that couldn't possibly be single." Betty hung her purse on the back of her chair and sat down. She smiled across the table at Elaine. "Hi. I probably should have started with that."

Elaine laughed. "Hi. How are you?"

"Good. Great, actually," she said. "Starving."

"Me, too. If you're in the mood for brunch, you can't go wrong with the quiche."

"I haven't had a quiche since I was a kid," Betty said. "I think my mom put everything humanly possible in quiche-form for a good couple years in the eighties."

"Well, if you don't want a traumatic childhood flashback, then they also have great burgers." Elaine pointed to a picture in the menu. "The kale burger with truffle mac and cheese is amazing."

Betty sat down her menu without even opening it. "I'm sold. To hell with my diet, right? I'm visiting an old friend. Today is a celebration."

Elaine's worries about the lunch with Betty faded to the background. And once they waded through the customary small talk and dug into all of the work drama Elaine had missed after she'd left the clinic, her worries disappeared entirely.

"Joanne was fired?" Elaine asked, her bite of scrambled eggs hanging perilously from the end of her fork, all but forgotten.

Betty suppressed a grin and nodded. "Management didn't have a choice. She slept with one of her clients!"

"And got pregnant." Elaine shook her head. "My goodness. Who told Bob?"

"Her husband is the one who found it all out. He showed up with flowers and lunch to surprise her on their anniversary."

Elaine gasped. "It was their *anniversary?*"

Betty nodded solemnly. "He walked in on a lot more than a therapy session, if you know what I mean."

Elaine shuddered. "Horrible. I can't imagine. Poor man."

"Poor me, too," Betty said. "I had to on-load half of her patients into my schedule. I don't think I left my office for a month."

"They didn't have doctors on reserve to fill the gaps?" When Elaine was office manager, she'd kept a file of therapists they could call in a pinch to fill any sudden openings. It had come in handy more than once.

"No. The office manager they hired after you left was a mess. Amber." Betty rolled her eyes. "She was the CEO's niece. Nepotism at its finest."

Elaine finally ate her eggs, now cold, and leaned back in her chair. "I've missed this, you know," she remarked, waving her hand back and forth between the two of them.

"I've missed *you*," Betty said. "I could talk office gossip with other people at the clinic. Although, loose lips sunk a lot of ships around there. But you were the only coworker I actually liked."

Elaine warmed. "I feel the same way. I should have kept in touch, but… you know how it goes."

"Not really," Betty said. "Not specifically, anyway. What has been going on? You mentioned you're renting out properties."

"Property. Singular," Elaine corrected. "Just a few of my upstairs rooms."

"Oh! And how does John feel about that?"

There it was: the elephant Betty didn't know was in the room. Bringing John up in the grocery store the day before had felt strange, but now it felt even more uncomfortable. Like she was trying to keep John a secret. Or worse, like his passing hadn't really affected her much.

Elaine steeled herself. "Actually, John passed. It's just me now."

Betty's eyes pinched together in sympathy. Elaine knew the look well. She'd seen her fair share of it the last few years.

"It's okay," she said quickly. "It's been three years now. So not terribly recent. Um… I'm doing okay, so—"

"Elaine," Betty said softly, "I'm so sorry. He was a really wonderful man."

A lump formed in her throat, and Elaine barely swallowed it down. "Thanks. He was."

"How are you?"

"I'm fine. The rental situation is—"

Betty shook her head and leaned forward. "How are *you*?"

Elaine blinked. She knew what Betty meant, but she didn't know how to respond. So few people had asked the question with such open sincerity that she didn't have a practiced answer ready.

Right after John passed, people reached out, of course. Friends and family checked in on her, and Elaine told them all she needed time. And they gave it to her. By the time Elaine was ready to talk, people had moved on. Elaine couldn't really blame them. They all had their own stuff going on.

But that didn't mean it wasn't hard.

Now, someone was checking in on her, and Elaine hardly knew how to act.

"I told you, I'm—"

"Liar." Betty gave her a sad smile. "Either that, or you're superhuman. Because I'd be a mess, let me tell you."

Maybe some people would have been offended by Betty's bluntness, but immediately, Elaine felt a weight lift off her shoulders.

Tears blurred her vision. "Maybe I'm kind of a mess."

Betty patted her hand. "There there, honey."

"But I'm okay, too," Elaine said, swiping at her eyes. "I miss him so much, and I feel like I've barely put my life back together. But I *have* put it back together. A bit. It's just... hard."

"Impossibly hard, I'm sure," Betty said. "Are the rentals part of putting things back together?"

Elaine shrugged. "I needed the money, to be honest. John and I retired early, so there are all kinds of rules about how much of his money I can receive. Basically, things didn't quite go according to plan. I was looking at selling the house if I didn't figure out how to make some extra money."

"Renting is smart. Lots of people are looking for a room for a week or so. And you're still in the same house, right? By the water?"

"Yeah, same house."

"I bet people love that," she said. "Hopefully you're charging enough. The biggest thing is to know what you're worth. Or what your property is worth, in this case."

That was a fair point. She probably wasn't charging enough. Especially since she was making Finn dinner most nights. But those dinners were a treat for Elaine, too. If she charged him for them, he might stop eating with her.

"I'm still working on the pricing and amenities and all of that," Elaine said. "I'm taking it slow. Gregory's girlfriend, Annette, is actually a friend of mine. She is more of a roommate than a renter, really."

"Oh, that's nice that you have a bit of company."

"Yeah, it is. For a while there, things were—" Without warning, Elaine's voice cracked. That lump in her throat was back. "Things were, um… lonely."

"Honey," Betty cooed. More often than not, Elaine found pet names annoying, but with Betty, it felt nice. "I'm really not going to harp on about this, but I wish you would have called me like you said you would."

"I never wanted to burden anyone else with my problems."

Betty swatted gently at her hand. "You are not a burden!"

Elaine couldn't respond. She'd been trying in vain to internalize that lesson, but it was harder than it seemed.

"And listen," Betty said, "it takes two to tango. Believe me, I know."

"Right," Elaine laughed. "Dance instructor and all."

"Exactly. I could have called you, and I didn't. But you can bet I will now."

Elaine swiped the last of her tears away. "Thanks, Betty."

"Of course," she said. "And if you're looking for a great group of girls, my dance classes are always looking for—"

"Oh no." She shuddered. "Not for me."

"Come on!" Betty prodded. "You never know until you give it a try."

Elaine chuckled. "I know, but trust me, you don't want me out there on a dancefloor. I'm a safety hazard."

Betty held up her hands in surrender. "Fine. Then we'll start with regular lunches."

"Start and *end* with lunches," Elaine clarified. "Hell will freeze over before you get me out there stepping to an eight-count."

"You say that now, but—"

"If this lunch is just a ruse to get me into your dance class, I'm afraid you're wasting your time."

It was only a joke, but Betty grew slightly more serious. "I could care less about the dance class. This lunch is a ruse to get you in my life again."

Elaine sobered, took a deep breath, and smiled. "Well, ruse successful then. It's good to see you, Betty."

"Good to see you, too, darling. We'll have you pirouetting in no time."

14

THE NEXT DAY AT ELAINE'S HOUSE

When was the last time she'd paid a bill in full? Elaine honestly couldn't remember. Usually, it was bare minimums and scraping by.

But today, she proudly signed her name at the bottom of her mortgage check.

"Someone looks awfully cheery." Annette walked into the kitchen and grabbed her water bottle out of the fridge. Elaine had given her the recipe for her favorite nausea cure-all—half a lemon and a knob of ginger soaked in water all night long. "What's going on in here?"

"Bills."

Annette wrinkled her nose. "Gotta be honest, that is not what I thought you were going to say."

Elaine laughed and closed her checkbook. "Why not be in a good mood? It's Saturday and the weather is perfect. What is there to be upset about?"

"Okay." Annette looked more than a little suspicious. "So do you have anything other than bills lined up for today?"

"Not a thing."

A wide-open Saturday used to feel like a black hole. Elaine would end up puttering around the house all day, trying to ignore the feeling that the world was spinning on without her. But if the last few weeks had taught her anything, it was that she could take control of these days.

"Actually, I was thinking about baking something," she said. "Do you know what Charlene likes? I was going to drop something off for her. I haven't heard anything from her in a few days."

Annette frowned. "That makes two of us. I think she's holing up a bit."

"Uh-oh. I thought about texting her… about Margaret and everything. I just didn't want to intrude."

"Do you have any recipes with white chocolate or raspberry?" Annette asked suddenly.

"Are you having another pregnancy craving? Because I still have an entire two-liter of unopened cream soda in the fridge."

"No. Well—yes. Always," Annette laughed. "But those are some of Charlene's favorites. Bake her something with raspberry and white chocolate and she'll come out of her hole for sure."

"That's great to know. Thank you!"

"And, I mean," Annette added, "if you happen to be at the store anyway and see those animal crackers with the pink and white frosting—well, I wouldn't turn my nose up at them."

After her fourth trip to the grocery store in as many days, Elaine made it home with everything she needed for the cake, plus a family-size bag of frosted animal crackers. And two hours after that, she had a moderately not-terrible looking cake.

Luckily, Charlene's house wasn't far. Transporting a Bundt cake by herself was no simple task. Elaine nearly overturned the thing twice on the way to the car. The heat wasn't helping matters, either. White chocolate frosting was not a fan of South Carolina's humidity.

By the time she knocked on Charlene's front door, she could see frosting beginning to pool in the center of the cake. As soon as the door opened, Elaine skipped friendly greetings and hurried into the air conditioning.

"I'm sorry to barge in, but this cake is about to be a puddle. Can I put it in the fridge?"

Charlene was clearly startled, but she gestured to the kitchen. "Of course. Go ahead."

Only once the cake was in the refrigerator did Elaine turn to her friend with a sigh. "Sorry about that. Hi."

"Hello," Charlene chuckled. "What was that about?"

"I wanted to bake you something. It's a raspberry Bundt cake with white chocolate frosting. Unfortunately, it was basically melting in my hands on the porch. Sorry for breaking into your house."

"Wow, thanks, Elaine. That sounds delicious. And I broke into your house first. Fair is fair."

That seemed like as good a segue as Elaine was going to get. "We actually haven't seen each other since then. I've missed you the past couple mornings on my walk."

"Yeah." Charlene dipped her head. "I'm sorry. I haven't been—"

"Don't apologize! I've just been a little worried."

"Sorr—er, I mean, I'm sorry you were worried, anyway. But I've been a little out of sorts. Trying to deal with what to do about Margaret without Tyler finding out what is going on is... it's a lot."

"Oh dear, how silly of me. I hadn't even thought about Tyler."

Margaret was the boy's mother. His birth mother, anyway. He was too young to understand the finer points of her situation, so it was probably best to keep him out of it altogether.

Charlene nodded solemnly. "He's still so shaken up about Annette moving out and Noah moving in. I don't want this to confuse him even more."

"That makes sense," Elaine said. "You're a really good mom."

Immediately, Charlene's eyes brimmed with tears. "Am I, though?"

"Of course you are!"

Charlene waved Elaine away. "You don't have to answer that. I'm being silly. I just... I feel like I have to choose between Margaret and Tyler sometimes. Like... like I can't love them both at the same time. Whatever is best for one isn't best for the other and it's hard because—"

"Because they're both your kids."

"Exactly," Charlene murmured.

It was obvious that a raspberry white chocolate cake was not going to be enough of a pick-me-up for this situation. "Do you want me to take Tyler for a little bit? I could get him out of the house. Give you time to put things in order."

Charlene shook her head. "No, you don't need to do that. I'm fine. Just being a little dramatic."

"Are you sure? You're not being dramatic and it wouldn't be any trouble."

"Yes, I'm—"

"Not sure at all," a deep voice interrupted.

Elaine turned around and saw Noah standing in the doorway. He wore a stern frown, the brunt of which was directed at his fiancé.

"I'm fine," Charlene breathed.

"Fine, maybe. But not great. Not awesome," Noah said. "Why don't you let Elaine help? Tyler would love to get out of the house."

"I know he would, but... if he's gone, I'm not sure what I'll do," Charlene admitted. "He's my little distraction."

Noah stepped in front of Charlene and pulled her in for a sweet hug. "Let me be your distraction. We'll take the boat out."

Elaine could see an excuse brewing on Charlene's face, so she stepped in before it could fully form. "That sounds so fun. And I'll take Tyler to the beach. Y'all haven't been there the last few mornings, so I'm sure he's missing it."

"There. It's settled," Noah said.

Charlene's mouth twisted to the side. She looked anything but settled.

"Okay," she relented. "I guess it's settled."

Elaine gave her an encouraging smile. "This will be fun."

That Afternoon At The Beach

"Maybe it's about time to head back to the house?" Elaine said gently.

Really, it was about two hours past time to head back to the house. Annette and Finn had their own keys to the front door, and Elaine knew they were both more than capable of feeding themselves, but she still liked to be there. She didn't know how to take off her "hostess" hat.

Tyler, however, could care less about any of that. The only thing that mattered to him was the hole he was digging in the sand.

"No!" he groaned. "Not yet. Just a little bit longer."

"It'll start getting dark soon. And we haven't eaten anything in a couple hours." Elaine was massively regretting the two measly granola bars she'd packed in the beach bag. "Aren't you hungry?"

"Nuh-uh." He tossed a garden shovel's worth of sand over his shoulder.

Elaine was debating whether she should tuck Tyler under her arm like a football and make a break for home when she looked down the beach to see three familiar outlines headed their way.

Annette threw a hand over her head and waved excitedly. Her other hand was firmly wrapped in Gregory's. Following along a few steps behind was Finn.

Once again, Elaine was shocked at how handsome her renter was. It was one thing to see him around the house. But when he was silhouetted against an orange sherbet sky with foamy surf brushing against his ankles, it was hard to forget this was real life and not the cover of a romance novel.

When they got close enough to talk, Elaine found herself a little tongue-tied. "Hey! What are you there?"

Annette chuckled. "What?"

Elaine pressed a palm to her forehead in embarrassment. "I meant, 'Hey there! What are you doing here?'"

"We're just out for a walk." Annette snuggled into Gregory's side.

Finn breezed past them to stand closer to Elaine. "And I tagged along. They were leaving as I was getting back for the day. Annette offered, and I couldn't say no."

"Annette wouldn't let him say no, is more like it," Gregory teased.

"Well, I knew Elaine and Tyler were down here. Charlene told me when I talked to her," she explained. "And this sunset is too beautiful to see it alone. It has to be shared."

"You're not wrong there. It's beautiful." Finn turned towards the water, and Annette shot Elaine a pointed look behind his back.

No matter how many times Elaine told her that Finn was nothing more than a friendly renter, Annette didn't seem able to let go of the idea of something romantic happening.

Elaine slowly shook her head, but Annette was already grinning as she stepped away from Elaine and Finn, dragging Gregory with her. Maybe Elaine was imagining things, but she thought Gregory tossed her a sympathetic shoulder shrug.

"Where's my nephew?" Annette growled playfully.

Tyler held out his little shovel like a weapon and giggled. "Nowhere!"

"Nowhere? Then who said 'nowhere'?"

"Nobody," he squealed.

Gregory gasped melodramatically and pointed at Tyler. "Annette, look! I found Nobody. There he is!"

Tyler took off sprinting and cackling through the sand as Annette and Gregory chased after him.

"That's cute," Finn chuckled.

"Adorable."

"I've never been very good with kids. I like them, though."

"Truer words have never been spoken," she sighed. Elaine sat down on the sand and Finn sat next to her, a respectable amount of space between them. "I mean, I love Tyler. I think he's the greatest kid I've ever met. But he probably sees me as some boring, weird neighbor lady."

Finn laughed out loud. "You don't really believe that, do you?"

"Hey, kids are ruthless. I'd be honored if that's the worst thing he thought about me." Elaine smiled. "I don't care either way. It's nice to spend time with him. Little ones teach you not to take yourself so seriously. Anything can be solved with a snack and a nap."

"I'll have to remember that. Next time I get a rejection letter, I'll eat a snack and take a nap."

"Is that a normal part of the job? Rejection letters?" Elaine asked.

"Oh, yeah," Finn said. "Unfortunately. But you get used to it. Plus, that's just one tiny con in the face of a million pros."

"Like what?"

"Travel and good food, for starters," he said. "And making my own hours is usually nice."

"Usually?"

Finn leaned in, a hand pressed to the side of his mouth like he was telling a secret. "Sometimes, I'm a bit of a procrastinator. And sometimes, I get distracted watching television or doing my laundry. Or going for a walk on the beach instead of submitting an outline to my editor."

Elaine laughed. "Oh no. Am I distracting you right now?"

"No, I'm distracting myself," he clarified. "Believe me, I wouldn't be here if I didn't want to be."

Warmth spread under Elaine's skin, even though she knew she was being silly. He just meant he wanted to be at the beach, of course.

There was a distant scream, and Elaine looked up. Gregory was chasing Tyler around in circles, a crab in his outstretched hand.

"Save me, Aunt Net!" Tyler bellowed. "It's gonna chomp me!"

Annette lazily stuck out a leg to trip Gregory, and he did a practiced tuck and roll in the sand. Tyler ran over and sat on his chest, a celebratory fist pumping in the air.

"Who wouldn't want to be here?" Elaine said, mostly to herself. "The beach is probably my favorite place in the world."

"Is that why you moved here?" he asked.

"Of course. You have to love where you live."

"Not necessarily. A lot of people don't."

"Hm. I guess that's true, but…" She shook her head. "I couldn't imagine not loving where I live. But that's probably because I don't travel as much as you do. If I did, maybe it wouldn't matter."

"Well, if you ever decided to start traveling, I know a guy who might be able to give you a few recommendations."

"I actually—when you made the reservation for the room and sent the letter, well, I… I looked you up."

"That makes sense," Finn said. "You can't have a stranger living in your house without knowing something about him."

"Yeah, right," she fumbled. "I read a few of your articles. They were good. Really good."

He smirked and nudged her elbow. "Catch a little inspiration, maybe?"

"Maybe," she admitted. "John and I always wanted to travel, but we never seemed to find the time. We thought we'd have more time when we retired, but then he—things changed."

"Things have a way of doing that, don't they?"

"Unfortunately," Elaine said.

Birds flew low over the water. Elaine could see chartered fishing boats and sailboats against the horizon, heading back to shore. It was getting late and she was still hungry, though those minor concerns didn't seem quite as pressing anymore. The sunset really was beautiful. And Annette was right: having someone to share it with made it even that much better.

"But sometimes," Finn said quietly, "change can be nice, too. Can't it?"

It was almost like he'd been reading her mind. Elaine swallowed down her surprise and nodded. "Yes. Yes, it can be. Sometimes."

15

THAT NIGHT AT CHARLENE'S HOUSE

Tyler was asleep on Elaine's shoulder when she knocked on Charlene's front door. Noah answered.

Hi, she mouthed, not wanting to wake the little boy up.

His sleep had been hard-won. Elaine was going to be sore tomorrow from running up and down the beach all day. And she couldn't remember the last time she'd eaten macaroni and cheese and hotdogs. But Tyler was well-fed and exhausted, and she hoped it would be a help to Charlene.

Noah's mouth fell open in shock when he realized Tyler was softly snoring. He immediately waved Elaine inside and led her up the stairs to Tyler's room.

A domed lamp sat on his bedside table. Glowing fish and whales swam across the walls and ceiling as it spun. His dark blue comforter was embroidered with green turtles and colorful starfish. It was an undersea wonderland.

"Just lay him down in his clothes," Noah whispered, pulling back the blankets on Tyler's big boy bed. "No pajamas tonight."

Luckily, Annette had changed him out of his sandy beach clothes back at the house. Even if she hadn't, though, Elaine guessed Noah would have said the same thing. People always say not to wake a sleeping baby, but waking a sleeping toddler is worse.

Elaine laid Tyler down and backed out of the room. Noah followed a second later, turning the handle slowly to silently release the latch. They didn't talk until they were safely downstairs.

"Thanks for that," Noah said. "To be honest, I'm starting to dread bedtime."

Elaine waved away his thanks. "My pleasure. It was fun to wear him out. How was the boat?"

Noah frowned. "I wish I knew. We didn't make it out today."

"Oh no. What happened?"

"Margaret," Noah said quietly. "Charlene got a call right after you left. She wasn't in any shape to get out of the house."

Elaine pressed a hand to her chest. "Is she okay? What happened?"

"Margaret pleaded guilty to the charges against her, and the judge sentenced her to jail time or rehab."

"Jail or rehab?" Elaine asked. "She gets a choice?"

Noah nodded. "Apparently. She wants to choose rehab."

"Who wouldn't? But that's a good thing, isn't it?"

"Maybe. But they've been down this road before. Margaret said she was going to get her act together once before, but it was all a scam. Charlene is hesitant to have any hope."

"Poor Charlene."

"Yeah," Noah agreed. "The real trouble is, Margaret called today… looking for a place to stay once rehab is over."

Elaine gasped. "She is going to come back and live with you all?"

"That's the big decision we have to make. Well," Noah amended, "the big decision Charlene has to make. I'm going to support whatever she chooses. Because it's tearing her up. She's worried about Margaret, but she also doesn't think it would be healthy for Margaret and Tyler to live under the same roof. Tyler is confused enough as it is."

Just that morning Charlene had said it was hard to be a good mom to both of her kids at the same time. And now, life had handed her a literal fork in the road. She couldn't do the best thing for everyone.

She'd have to choose.

"That's an impossible choice," Elaine said. "Bless her heart. I'm so sorry."

Noah gave her a sad smile. "I'll pass it along. Thanks for being such a good friend to her. She needed Tyler out of the house today. But she needed me, too. I didn't know what I was going to do."

"Call me anytime, Noah. Seriously. If either of you need anything, call me. I'm right up the road."

"Thanks, Elaine. Have a good night."

When she got home, Elaine was so wrapped up in worry for Charlene and Tyler that she didn't see Finn sitting on the front porch until she was almost on top of him.

"Evenin', roomie," he drawled in a terrible stereotypical Southern accent.

Elaine yelped. "Oh my word! You scared me."

"Sorry," he chuckled. "I tried to wave as you walked up so you'd see me, but you seemed pretty focused."

Her heart was still pattering against her ribs, but it was beginning to slow a bit as she took up the chair next to Finn's. "I was in my own world. And I'm jumpy, anyway. It's a curse."

"I'll remember that. No tip-toeing around the house."

"Exactly. Please don't. People always complain about people stomping around the house, but I kind of like it. It's comforting to know you're up there."

Finn gave her a curious look, and heat spread down Elaine's back.

"Or, you know, to know that someone is up there. Anyone." She cleared her throat. "To know I'm not alone."

"That makes sense. I've never minded being on my own. But that's mostly because of the way I grew up."

"Big family?" Elaine asked.

"Not so much. I have one sister and a brother, but they were both out of the house by the time I was six or seven."

"Were you a surprise baby, then?"

"You could say that." Finn chuckled darkly. "My parents weren't really... the parenting type. I'm not sure they meant to have any of us, to be honest."

Elaine didn't know what to say, and Finn must have picked up on that.

"I'm fine, don't get me wrong," he added. "Well-adjusted and all that. Plus, I think I'm a bit too old for childhood trauma to still be a factor, don't you?"

Trauma? Finn was so warm and friendly it was hard to imagine his childhood as anything less than a Norman Rockwell painting.

"I don't think it's called 'childhood trauma' because you outgrow it," Elaine said. "I think it's just trauma. And there's no expiration date on that."

He smiled, but it looked more like a wince. "You're probably right. Especially since I still can't even handle seeing my family. I don't think I've been home in... ten years? Probably longer."

"Considering your job, I doubt airfare is the thing holding you back."

"Definitely not. I have so many points I might actually be partial owner of the airline," he joked. "It's not that. It's just… my parents are addicts. Have been my whole life. So is my brother."

Words lodged in her throat. Elaine played back the last couple minutes, trying to decide if she'd said anything insensitive. If she'd known what Finn was carrying, she wouldn't have been so flippant.

"I'm so sorry." It was all she could think to say.

"Thanks," he said softly. "I don't like to talk about them much. It's just… hard. I still love them, but I can't be the person trying to fix things all the time."

"What about your sister?" Elaine asked. "You mentioned your parents and brother, but—"

"She died when I was twelve. Overdose."

Elaine's heart sank. "I'm so sorry." She was starting to sound like a broken record.

"Me, too," he said. "I thought maybe that would clean my parents up, but it didn't change anything. When I was old enough, I tried helping my brother. I thought maybe I could get through to him, but…"

"What did you try?"

Finn looked over at her, something like suspicion in his eyes.

"I don't mean to pry," she said quickly. "It's just… you know Annette— well, of course you do. But anyway, her sister, Charlene, has a daughter who is struggling with addiction. I want to help, but I'm not sure what to say or do."

He visibly relaxed. "Oh. Well, judging by my family's track record, I don't know what to say or do, either."

"Right. Yeah. Sorry." Elaine's voice trailed off. She could practically feel stars dropping off the review Finn was going to leave her rental. If he did write about his experience staying there in his book, it would probably involve a nosey, insensitive host.

Finn leaned forward and caught her eyes. "I'm sorry. I'm not great at talking about my family yet. Or my failures. And trying to help my brother was a failure in a major way."

"You don't have to talk about it."

"I want to," he assured her. "Or, I need to, anyway. And if it could help Charlene's daughter... maybe it would be worth putting it all out there."

Elaine didn't know what to say, so she reached out and patted his shoulder. "She'd appreciate it. I would, too. We're fish out of water here."

Finn nodded. "It's a different world. Psychologically, anyway. The person you know—the person you grew up with and looked up to— they slip away. I could look at Aaron and see that he was my brother, but he didn't act like my brother. He was selfish and erratic. He lied to me, stole from me, used me. I wouldn't wish any of it on my worst enemy. The addiction or the role I played in it all."

"That's how Charlene describes Margaret." Elaine wanted to try and make Finn more comfortable. She wanted him to know he wasn't alone. "Tyler is actually Margaret's son, not Charlene's. She dropped him off on Charlene's doorstep over a year ago."

He whistled. "Well, isn't that something? I don't see how you could help anyone more than raising their child for them."

"She just got arrested again," Elaine explained. "She has to go to rehab, and when it's over, she wants to move in with her mom. I guess she's looking for some stability."

"Hopefully." Finn's expression looked far from convinced.

"Hopefully," Elaine echoed. "But needless to say, Charlene is worried about how Tyler will handle all of it. He's dealing with some trauma of his own—abandonment and all that—so she isn't sure having Margaret around all the time will be good for him."

"That makes lots of sense to me."

"And I want to help, but I don't have any experience with any of this," Elaine sighed. "I don't have kids, I've never been close to an addict. I just don't know what to do or say."

"Well, you're doing and saying all the right stuff now." He smiled at her. "I think you're better at this than you think you are."

"I was the office manager at a mental health clinic for a long time. Maybe I picked up a trick or two over the years being around all those smart people."

"Well, I'm by no means a professional," he said. "But I can tell you that I would feel worse right now if I'd never tried to help my brother."

"Even though it failed?" She winced. "Sorry, that sounded awfully insensitive. I just mean—"

"It's fine, seriously. It was a failure. But *I'm* not a failure. Does that make sense?"

Elaine scrunched up her nose. "I think so."

Finn took a deep breath. "I never had the power to succeed or fail where my brother was concerned. All I could do was try to give him the opportunity to get better. Just because he didn't get better doesn't mean I failed. Really... I succeeded. I did my best. And that's all I could do."

"That makes sense." Elaine elbowed him gently. "I think you're better at this than you think you are, too. Seems like you know exactly what to say."

He grinned. "People tell me I have a way with words."

"They're not wrong."

He rose to his feet with a groan. "Well, it's late for me. I did a walking tour today, and I think I about wore through my shoes. I'm sore."

"I'm with you. Chasing a four-year-old around the beach should be an Olympic event."

Finn smiled. "You said earlier you weren't good with kids, but you're great with Tyler. You seem to be great with everyone, actually. Old and young alike."

"Good to hear I'm a crowd-pleaser," Elaine chuckled nervously.

"You are," he said earnestly. "You're here talking to me, trying to find ways to help your friend with her family drama. It's admirable how much you care."

The conversation had taken a personal turn. It was easy to talk about someone else's problems. They were a step removed. But talking about what was going on in her head and her life? A whole different story.

"Lord knows I certainly try to."

"That's all you can do. And that's what I'd tell Charlene, too: just try. But don't sacrifice yourself in the process."

Elaine frowned. "Hm."

"Sometimes, we get so caught up taking care of everyone around us, we forget to take care of ourselves." Finn looked down at her, and Elaine couldn't help but feel like it was a bit pointed. "You can't light a candle with a burnt-out match."

Then Finn left her, with a smile and a head full of thoughts.

16

THE NEXT DAY AT ELAINE'S HOUSE

"We should get this on the schedule," Annette said. "Once a week we get together. 'The Whine and Cheese Club': how's that for a name?"

Charlene scoffed. "You won't have anything on your schedule once the little one gets here. Not unless it involves feeding, rocking, or changing a baby."

Annette swirled the apple juice in her glass. "You have time for this, and you have Tyler."

"He's four," Charlene said. "Newborns are different."

Elaine leaned over and patted Annette's shoulder. "I'll help you out. I love to babysit, and I'm right down the hall. And for Tyler, I'm just down the street. Bring on the kiddos, I say."

"And I'll help, too," Charlene offered. "But no one can sub in for Mom in those earlier days. Babies can smell their moms. They need you. Like it or not, that little babe is going to be strapped to you for at least a year."

Annette took a long drink in lieu of a retort. Elaine could tell she was doing her best to ignore her sister's pessimistic view. Which made sense, seeing as how Charlene was in a bit of a mood. It was understandable given everything going on, but difficult to deal with, since Charlene also didn't want to talk about Margaret.

She'd made that clear. "I'm here to forget," she'd said as soon as Annette had opened the door. "Noah has Tyler tonight, and I'm here to hang with the girls and relax. Okay?"

Except, she didn't seem relaxed.

"For Margaret, it was longer," Charlene mused. "Might end up being forever. Who knows?"

Annette and Elaine locked eyes, a silent conversation passing between them in just one look.

Someone needed to talk to Charlene. The elephant in the room was stomping all over their good time.

"Hey, Char," Annette said sweetly. Too sweetly. Charlene was suspicious from the outset.

She narrowed her eyes. "What?"

"Um. Well, I wonder if maybe talking about… Margaret—maybe that would make you feel better? You seem a little—"

"I'm fine."

Annette rolled her eyes and tipped her head towards Elaine. The message was clear: *I tap out. Your turn.*

Elaine nodded gently. She'd give it her best try.

"Sometimes, the best way to forget your problems for a little bit is to talk them through first," Elaine suggested. "That's why people go to therapy, right? Because their problems are easier to deal with after they talk with someone."

Charlene sat up straighter. "I don't need to go to therapy."

Swing and a miss. Finn had misjudged her the night before: Elaine was not great at talking to people.

"No one is saying you do," Annette chimed in hurriedly. "But even if you did, that's fine. Tyler goes, doesn't he?"

"Yeah." Charlene ran a finger around the rim of her glass, mulling something over. Finally, she sagged into the sofa. "I actually emailed his therapist and told her about what is going on. I don't want her to bring up specifics with Tyler, but I wondered if maybe she could start seeding some things into their chats that might help him... process? I don't know."

"Does that mean you're going to let Margaret come live with y'all?" Annette asked.

Charlene shrugged. "I have no idea. I've talked my way around the idea a thousand times, but I still have no clue what to do. No clue what's right."

"I don't think there is any one right answer," Elaine offered.

Annette nodded in agreement. "That's true. This isn't a trivia game. It's life."

"Is there a difference?" Charlene chuckled bitterly. "Feels like life has been just a series of hard choices the last few years."

"But you've handled them all gracefully." Elaine cleared her throat. "I've never come right out and said it, but... I admire you, Charlene."

"Oh, Elaine. You don't have to—"

"I know," she said. "I'm not saying it because I have to. Or because I want to make you feel better. It's just true. I admire how you've handled everything since Davy died."

Charlene pressed her lips together into a thin line. "Thanks."

"I know what that's like," Elaine continued. "John died just a couple years after Davy passed. The world stopped, you know? But I'd seen you handle it, and I thought I would be the same. I thought I'd just pick up and carry on the way you did. With your business and your life. But then it was my turn, and wow… it's not nearly as easy as you made it look. I couldn't do it."

Annette squeezed Elaine's shoulders. "You did fine. There's no one way to grieve."

"You're right," Elaine said. "And this isn't about me. I don't want it to be about me. I just… I know that if anyone is equipped to make a decision and see it through, it's you, Charlene."

Being vulnerable was new. Elaine held her breath while she waited for Charlene to say something. Anything.

Then she heard a sniffle.

Charlene swiped at her eyes. "Darn it. I'm not supposed to be crying tonight."

"Goodness, I'm sorry," Elaine sighed. "I thought—"

"It's fine. It's good, actually," Charlene said.

"Good crying?"

"Yeah. I needed it. Thank you, Elaine. This is better than forgetting."

"That's great." Elaine swelled with relief. "Not the crying, but the— You know what I mean. But I'm glad you said that, because I actually wanted to talk to you about something."

Charlene waved her on. "We've come this far. Might as well keep going."

"I don't want to overstep, but I've been so worried about you and Margaret and Tyler, and I… I took it upon myself to do a little bit of research."

With both Annette's and Charlene's attention on her, Elaine felt flushed. Though it also could have been the wine. One glass was her usual limit, and she was onto her third. She was feeling loose.

"Margaret asked to stay with you after rehab, and whatever you decide will be fine. I don't want you to feel like I'm trying to tell you how to take care of your child. But I was looking online last night and found a lot of different resources locally. There are programs and meetings. But there are also halfway houses where Margaret could live."

Charlene wrinkled her nose. "Aren't those for criminals?"

"Well… she is a criminal," Annette said. Charlene swatted her arm, and Annette held up her hands in surrender. "Sorry, but she is!"

"Yeah, but I don't want her living amongst them," Charlene argued. "You are the company you keep. Which is probably why I find myself becoming more and more immature by the day."

It was Annette's turn to swat at her sister. "I'm only this way around you. I swear, I'm a mature adult the rest of the time."

Elaine laughed. Together, they really did revert back to what Elaine imagined was their teenage selves.

"She'd be in a specific house for addicts. They wouldn't place her with violent criminals or anyone charged with serious offenses. It would be a group of people who are all looking to get better. And I just thought maybe that would be a better fit for you all."

Charlene sighed. "You might be right. When Margaret ran away, I swore I'd do anything to get her home again. But now… well, now I'm not sure it's what is best. She needs to learn how to manage this and stand on her own two feet. Plus, there's Tyler."

"He has barely adjusted to me moving out," Annette said. "I can't imagine how he'll handle his mom reappearing all of the sudden."

"I know," Charlene agreed. "He doesn't really understand drugs or addiction, but I've tried to explain things to him. I told him his mom has problems that keep her away. If she comes back, I'm worried he'll think she's there to stay. And, well, with her track record, I can't promise that."

Something Finn said popped into Elaine's head. "You have no control over whether Margaret sobers up or not. It's not your decision to make. Or Tyler's. But if Margaret moves in with you and then falls off the wagon again, Tyler might not be able to understand that it isn't because of him."

Charlene nodded. "Exactly. That's exactly it, Elaine. You nailed it."

"Well, I didn't nail it," she said. "Finn did. He has some family members who have dealt with addiction, so—"

"Finn?" Charlene frowned.

"My renter." Elaine hitched a thumb towards the ceiling, even though Finn wasn't in tonight. "He's doing a 'restaurant crawl' tonight. He said it was like a bar crawl, but I'm only vaguely familiar with what that is, so—"

"You told him about Margaret?" Charlene interrupted. "About what's going on with us?"

Elaine blinked. "Um. Well, yeah. We were talking last night about our families, and he mentioned that there is addiction in his family."

Charlene set her glass down and straightened up. "So, you told him about my family?"

Elaine couldn't tell if she'd done something wrong. She looked to Annette for some kind of clue, but Annette was gawking at Charlene, too.

"Well, I'd just been so worried about you and everything going on. I wanted to help, so I asked him if he had any advice. It really wasn't a big deal, I promise."

Charlene stood up. "My family is actually a very big deal to me, Elaine."

"I know! Of course I know that. That isn't what I meant."

Annette chimed in. "Yeah, I don't think she meant to—"

"I didn't even tell you about Margaret until I had to," Charlene said. "I didn't tell Annette. I didn't tell anyone until Tyler showed up on my doorstep. What makes you think you can share that information with people I don't know?"

Elaine's heart hammered in her chest. She'd done something wrong. That much was obvious. Now, she needed to fix it.

"Finn is a good guy," she said. "I'll explain things to him. He won't tell anyone."

"He's the writer, isn't he?" Charlene asked.

"He's a travel writer."

"But he's working on an article or something—"

"A book," Elaine said. "He's writing about—"

"About his time in Isle of Palms," Charlene interrupted. "About the places he saw and the people he met. About the landlord who gossiped with him."

Hurt lanced through her. "I wasn't gossiping, Charlene. I was trying to help. I'm sorry if—"

"What if he writes about Margaret? Or Tyler?"

"He won't! Of course he won't."

"I wouldn't even blame him," Charlene continued, growing angrier with every word. "It's a great story. Juicy, really. Good enough to gossip about at the very least."

"Charlene, he won't. I promise. If you knew him, then—"

"You don't even know him!" Charlene grabbed her purse from under the coffee table. "I know you don't have a lot of other friends, Elaine. But you can't go around trusting people like this. It's naïve."

Elaine was so shocked she couldn't even speak.

But Annette could. She spoke gently. "Char, I know you're upset, but let's not—"

Charlene held up a hand to cut her sister off. "Please don't tell me what to do right now. Or how to feel."

"I wasn't going to," Annette said. "But—"

"I need to go." Charlene took a breath like maybe she was going to say something else. But then, all at once, she spun towards the door and walked out.

Elaine sat dumbstruck in her wake.

17

THE NEXT DAY AT ELAINE'S HOUSE

As soon as Elaine opened her eyes, it felt like she'd been hit over the head with a brick. Not just because she'd had too much to drink the night before, or because she'd fallen asleep crying, though both those things were true.

But because there was a brick-sized cat sitting on her head.

"Ghost!" She scooped the cat up with a groan and nestled him against her side. "I'm fine."

The cat meowed and nuzzled into the hand she was using to pet him.

"Or are you here because you're hungry?"

Elaine had slept in. Usually, she liked to be up and out of the house before the sun could even make it over the horizon. And since Finn and Annette moved in, she tried even harder to be downstairs to greet them when they came down each morning.

But today, she wasn't in the mood to greet anyone or walk anywhere.

Which meant she hadn't fed Ghost yet.

The cat cast a mournful look in her direction. If eyes were windows to the soul, Ghost's soul was made of kibble.

"Fine," she sighed. "Give me a second."

Elaine padded into her master bathroom and assessed the situation.

The wild hair she could deal with. Nothing a quick run through with the brush couldn't fix. She'd never exactly been one to style her hair anyway. And the older she got, the more it seemed to have a mind of its own.

But the puffy eyes and dark circles? That was going to be a problem.

After Charlene had stormed out, Annette had followed her without a word or look back to Elaine. It made sense. Charlene was her sister. Plus, Annette probably wanted to catch her before she made it all the way home. It would be easier to talk her down face-to-face.

But after fifteen minutes had passed without Annette coming back in, Elaine had crept to the front window to peek out at them. That's when she'd realized they were gone. And so was Charlene's car.

Another fifteen minutes later, she'd gotten the text from Annette that she was going to stay with Charlene for the night.

She's upset. She needs me.

For some reason, that text had opened the floodgates. Elaine was grateful Finn had been out late. Otherwise, he would've come home to find her puddled on the living room floor.

For a moment in the midst of her crying, she'd thought she wanted that. It would have been nice to have someone with her in that moment. Someone to talk to. She was upset in her own right.

But then, she'd remembered what Charlene had said. *You don't even know him.*

That wasn't true, was it?

Finn had told her about his family. About his own struggles. And he'd admitted he didn't talk about those things often. That spoke to a certain level of intimacy between them.

Elaine also knew about his job and his lifestyle. Sure, maybe she didn't know his favorite movies or if he had any allergies. But she knew the important things.

I know you don't have a lot of other friends, Elaine. But you can't go around trusting people like this. It's naïve.

The echo of Charlene's words sounded more biting in her head. Was she really naïve? Had her loneliness made her desperate, silly, thoughtless?

Ghost mewled, pulling her out of her head.

Elaine quickly swiped makeup under her eyes and stepped into a pair of pants. If she moved quickly, maybe no one would see her. But if Finn or Annette did catch her, at least she wouldn't look like she'd just rolled out of bed, as true as that may have been.

Ghost followed her down to the kitchen, curling around her ankles with excitement.

"I knew it," she chided. "You weren't worried about me at all."

The cat was shameless as she poured a cup of kibble into his bowl. He practically pounced on her hand before she could even finish.

Figured. No one seemed overly concerned about her.

She'd left her phone downstairs in the kitchen overnight, but when she checked it, she didn't have any missed calls or texts. Nothing at all from Annette or Charlene.

Had Annette been able to calm Charlene down? Should Elaine try to mend fences just yet?

Obviously, Charlene had been upset the night before. That's the only reason she'd made any comments about Elaine's social life—or lack thereof. Elaine knew that, but it did little to ease the sting. Every time she thought about it, she flushed with shame.

"I should be the bigger person," she mumbled to herself. "I should do the right thing."

Before she could talk herself out of it, Elaine tapped Charlene's name and pressed her phone to her ear.

I'm sorry, she thought. *I'm sorry.*

That's all she needed to say.

She just needed Charlene to know that she was sorry. And so long as that message came across, things would go back to normal. Charlene couldn't hold this against her forever, could she? After all, Elaine's intentions had been pure. She'd only been trying to help Margaret, and Charlene by extension.

But explanations don't matter right now. I'm sorry, she thought as it continued to ring. *I'm sorry.*

Then it went to voicemail.

Elaine wasn't prepared when she heard the beep, telling her to leave her message. This wasn't something she wanted to happen over a voicemail. Or a phone call, for that matter. This had been a horrible idea.

She hung up. But before she could even set her phone down, it vibrated. She thought it might be Charlene calling her back, but when she looked down, it was a text.

ANNETTE: *She isn't ready to talk. I'll talk to you when I get home tonight.*

Her heart sank.

Charlene had seen that she'd called, and ignored it. Then she'd had Annette text Elaine back. She couldn't even do it herself.

"How bad is this?" she muttered.

No one answered. Because there was no one there to answer.

The stuffy silence of her house was making her skin crawl more than it ever had before. She turned to head back upstairs with the vague thought of putting a record on for the background noise...

When she came face-to-face with John.

He smiled out of the frame the way he always did, hanging just above the dining room table. Elaine hadn't forgotten his picture was there, but she'd stopped looking for it every day. Since Finn and Elaine had shown up, she didn't need to see him to make it through another evening spent alone. To get her going on another quiet morning.

But now...

"I messed up, John." Tears ran down her cheeks. "I don't talk to anyone about you. About why I keep your picture above the table—so I wouldn't have to eat alone every night. No one knows I talk to you like you're still here. So why did I blab to Finn about Charlene's problems?"

Her intentions really had been good, but Charlene had every right to be upset. Elaine had broken her trust.

And why?

Because Finn was handsome. Because he kept her company at dinner time. Because she liked to hear him moving around upstairs, reminding her she wasn't alone.

"I'm sorry." Elaine didn't know if she was talking to Charlene or John. "I thought things would get better if I opened up our house. If I had people here again. But the problem wasn't that I was alone. The problem is that I don't know how to be around other people."

She felt the truth of it as she spoke.

"I know how to be with *you*," she whispered. "Or rather, I knew how to be with you. But everyone else? That was your area of expertise. Not mine.."

When it came to Mason and Judy—even Charlene and Davy the few times they'd hung out together as couples—John carried the conversation. People flocked to him. He was friendly and warm and knew how to draw people in.

"But I have to figure this out, John," she said. "I can't go back to the way things were. After you left—after you died, it was quiet. It felt like a tomb in here. And I have to figure out how to fix this. Because I can't go back to that."

Would Annette move out? If Charlene was truly angry with Elaine, if she'd done something unforgivable, how could Annette live with her? Charlene wouldn't come visit. Tyler probably wouldn't be allowed over anymore. Annette would move out, and then it would just be Elaine and a never-ending rotation of faceless, interchangeable renters.

"I can't do that." Elaine swiped at her eyes. "How do I fix this? What do I need to do?"

John smiled down at her, silent. As Elaine stared up, waiting for a response that would never come, she realized something about his face looked strange. Almost like a bad Photoshop job.

She stepped forward to get a better look and saw the problem: the picture had wrinkled.

It was a slight wrinkle, not even a crease. Just a little hump in the photo stock. But it was right over John's face. He looked more like Quasimodo than himself now.

And that was the final straw.

Elaine bent forward and sobbed.

A Few Days Later At Elaine's House

"Have I done something wrong?"

Elaine looked up from her dinner and saw Finn was looking at her. Concern creased his brow.

She hadn't invited him to eat dinner with her. When he'd walked through the front door and smelled her cooking, he'd invited himself.

"I caught you," he'd said. "Our schedules have been out of sync the last couple days."

That wasn't by accident. Elaine didn't know what to say to Finn, how to talk to him. Not after everything had happened.

The more Elaine sat with what she'd done, the worse she felt.

How could she have betrayed one of her oldest friends like this? Finn was a writer. He could probably even be considered a journalist. Was their conversation on the record? Elaine didn't even know what that meant. And she didn't want to ask.

She just wanted to pretend it had never happened.

But that was hard, since Charlene still wouldn't take her calls. Even Annette had been more distant than usual.

"Just busy at work," she'd explained the previous morning. She was holding the bottle of lemon and ginger water Elaine had made for her, which had seemed like a good sign. But it was hard to tell. "We'll sit down and chat soon, okay?"

Elaine had walked around for almost two days with a knot in her stomach, convinced she'd ruined everything. Apparently, Finn had taken notice.

"What?" Elaine asked.

"You seem upset," Finn said. "I don't want to be vain and assume it has something to do with me, but, well… it seems like it has something to do with me."

Elaine shook her head. "No, no. Everything is fine. I'm fine."

"Is it about your friend?" he asked. "I'm sorry, I forgot her name… Annette's sister—is it about her? Is everything okay?"

Shame washed through her again. He didn't even know Charlene's name, but he knew all of her secrets.

Then something occurred to her.

Was Finn fishing for more details? She hadn't wanted to believe Charlene's theory that Finn was going to write about her drama in his book, but maybe there was some truth to the idea. Maybe he was coming back to verify things before he wrote it down.

"She's fine," Elaine snapped. "I was being dramatic the other night."

He frowned. "You were being a good friend. I don't think that makes you dramatic. It means you care."

"Good friends don't gossip about their friends to reporters."

Finn leaned back. "What? Do you mean me?"

"Who else?" Elaine couldn't meet his eyes.

"I'm… I'm not a reporter," he stammered, taken aback. "Not like that, anyway. Do you think I'm going to write about this or something?"

Elaine waved her hands. "It's not my business what you write. You're here for a job, and I just need to remember that, that's all."

She carried her plate into the kitchen. This conversation needed to be over. The damage was done and there was no point rehashing it. Best to put it all behind them.

But Finn followed her. "Elaine," he breathed. "I'm a *travel* writer, for goodness' sake. I'm writing a guide book, basically. Where would I find room to gossip?"

She'd just used the word herself, but hearing Finn charge her with gossiping about Charlene still took her by surprise.

"It's none of my business," Elaine said. "That's what I've learned—to mind my own business. You're here for work, and I shouldn't be interrupting you, anyway."

Finn dropped his shoulders in a sigh. "I—I don't understand what happened. But I can promise you I'm not going to say anything to anyone about your friend, if that is what this is about."

"Charlene."

"What?"

"Her name is Charlene," Elaine said. "She's a dear friend of mine, and I shouldn't have told you anything about her."

"Okay."

"Okay," Elaine repeated.

She had been rinsing her plate in the sink for almost a minute, but Finn was still standing there. Not leaving. Why wasn't he leaving?

He walked around the island and stood next to her. A bit too close. She turned off the water and slid her plate into the dishwasher.

"It isn't my fault you told me about your friend," he said finally.

Elaine's jaw tightened. How could she both know he was right, but also still be angry with him? It was like her mind was operating on two different levels. One was rational, but the other, much more dominant part, blamed Finn for all of this.

"You're right. It isn't," she said. "It's mine. I just need to remember to be professional from here on out. You're a guest, not my friend."

Finn inhaled sharply. "I don't see why I can't be both."

"Because," Elaine swallowed. "… Because you just can't. You don't live here. You'll be leaving. I shouldn't have mixed business with—" The word *"pleasure"* popped into her mind, but it felt too intimate. "With my social life," she finished instead.

"You're saying we can't be friends?"

Elaine shrugged.

"That's ridiculous, Elaine."

"I don't see why it matters. We'll still see each other. I'll be friendly."

"Friendly, but not friends." He shook his head. "I don't understand any of this. I don't understand you."

And there it was. Yet more proof that Elaine didn't know how to deal with people. She'd always felt grateful for having John in her life, but maybe she hadn't been grateful enough. He understood her, seemed to know without a word shared between them what she was feeling. They were in sync—best friends—and Elaine didn't think she'd ever have that with anyone else.

"You may not understand, but I'd like you to respect my boundaries."

Finn stared at her. His square jaw clenched, and Elaine was ready to fight. To defend her decision. But then, in a sigh, he retreated.

"I'm not sure if I can do that," he admitted. "So maybe it would be best if I found a new place to stay."

This was what Elaine wanted, right? So why were tears burning at the backs of her eyes? Why was her throat clogged with emotion?

Finn seemed to wait for a response. But when one didn't come, he nodded to her. A silent goodbye.

Then, just like Charlene did, just like John did…

He left her alone.

18

THE NEXT DAY AT ELAINE'S HOUSE

"There you are!" Annette said, pushing the screen door closed behind her. "I didn't expect you to still be out here. Usually, you're buzzing around the house by now."

"I'm having a slow morning." Elaine sunk down further in her deck chair.

Really, she was hiding. From who, she didn't know. Finn had already packed up his room and left early that morning. Maybe she was hiding from herself. Hoping she could stare out at the sunset and let her mind wander somewhere else, somewhere far away from here.

"Me too." Annette slid a deck chair up next to Elaine's and plopped down with a sigh. "I have a doctor's appointment in an hour, so I took a half day."

"How are things going with you and the baby?"

Annette smiled and patted her stomach. "Good. I still have so much to sort out, so I don't want to rush anything really, but... it would be nice to have a bump. Having a little baby bump might make it feel more real."

"The nausea isn't doing that?" Elaine teased.

"Oh, it is," Annette scoffed. "But if I had a bump, maybe everyone else would be more sympathetic. I'd like to start getting some special treatment from strangers."

"I'll treat you special."

Annette nudged her elbow. "You already do, making me special water bottles every day. I appreciate it."

"Of course. Anything I can do to help."

They smiled at one another and then slipped into a strained silence.

This was the first time they'd really sat down since the disastrous Whine and Cheese Club night. Beyond a few text messages back and forth, they hadn't discussed anything of substance. Elaine still didn't really even know how Annette felt about it all.

Part of her didn't want to know.

"So, we should talk," Annette sighed.

Elaine's chest tightened. "Okay."

"Sorry I haven't been around. I'm sure that sounded like a line when I said it, but work really did get busy."

"I believed you." Elaine really hadn't, but there was no need to say so.

"Good," Annette said. "Because I really don't want to get in the middle of this... thing between you and Charlene."

It was a *thing*. She hated the sound of that. And she hated even more that it was all her fault.

"I don't want to put you in the middle. I don't even want to be in it myself," Elaine admitted.

"I know. But you do see where she is coming from... right?"

Elaine nodded. "Of course."

"Like I said, I don't want to pick sides, but… Charlene is really private," Annette said. "She only trusts a few people with her personal stuff. The only reason I knew anything was going on with Margaret was because Margaret had told me, in a roundabout way. Charlene never said a word."

"She didn't tell me until recently, either," Elaine said. "I wish she had, though. I would have tried to help."

Annette nodded. "So would I. But that doesn't change the fact that it's hard for Charlene to open up. And telling Finn everything, while well-intentioned, was… well, it wasn't what she wanted."

"I know. Gosh, I know."

Annette reached out and squeezed Elaine's shoulder. It was a small gesture, but there was tenderness in it. Elaine resisted the urge to lean over and pull Annette into the hug she so desperately needed.

"I'm not mad at you. Just to be clear," Annette said. "I know you were just trying to help. None of us know what we're doing here, and you were asking someone with experience. I can't be mad at you for caring about my sister enough to do that."

"Well, thank you, sweetheart. I needed to hear that."

"And…" Annette hesitated. "I'm sorry on Charlene's behalf, too."

"For what?"

"She was angry that night, and she said some things that were uncalled for, in my opinion."

Elaine shrugged. "She wasn't wrong, though. I don't have many friends."

"I mean… I guess that's true, if you say so, but still." Annette shook her head. "It wasn't fair for her to use that against you. Just because you keep your friend circle small doesn't mean you're naïve."

Elaine wasn't so sure. It felt like no matter how careful she was lately, she kept tripping all over herself.

"And Finn is really nice," Annette said. "You were right. If Charlene knew him, she wouldn't be so upset. He promised me he wouldn't say a word to anyone about Margaret."

"You talked to Finn?"

She nodded. "I caught him on his way out this morning. He seemed… upset."

Elaine chewed on her lower lip and didn't say anything.

"He told me he was leaving by choice, but he didn't seem happy about it," Annette continued. "It seemed like, maybe… maybe he felt his hand was forced."

"I didn't tell him to leave," Elaine said quickly.

"What did you tell him? If you don't mind me asking."

Elaine did mind, mostly because the topic still made her uncomfortable. But she was also desperate for someone to talk to about this. After three years, she was tired of pouring her heart out to a picture in a frame.

"I just told him we would be friendly, but not friends. That I should be more professional."

Annette hissed. "Ouch."

"What? Was that bad?" Guilt twisted her insides. "He's renting from me. I can't become friends with every person who wants to stay here."

"Why not?"

"Because… because…" Elaine dug around in her mind for a good reason, but came up empty. "He is going to leave. He's a travel writer. Long-distance friendships never work out."

"Finn is a really nice guy," Annette said. "And from what he's said to me, he doesn't seem interested in leaving the Lowcountry anytime soon. Maybe not ever, actually. He seems to have found some peace here."

"What makes you say that?"

"Because he told me he found some peace here," Annette chuckled. "He travels a lot, and I think it is hard for him to feel settled. But he said that he feels at home here. 'I like the people' were his exact words. I wouldn't be surprised if he decided to stay for good."

Elaine's heart thundered in her chest, but she didn't know why. What did it matter? Finn could live here if he wanted. She wasn't the gatekeeper of the Isle of Palms.

"But for now, he is renting one of those condos along Palm Boulevard."

Elaine knew exactly where Annette was referring to. The condos were cute, but very resort-like. Not at all what Finn had been looking for.

"Oh, that's nice," Elaine said.

Annette didn't say anything, but Elaine could feel her staring at her, almost as if she was searching for a reaction.

"I actually just noticed an osprey nest in that tree right over there," Elaine pointed out after the silence stretched a bit too long. "I'm always looking at the sunrise, so I never noticed, but it looks like it's been there for a while."

"Oh yeah, that's a big ol' girl," Annette remarked when she saw. "Pretty."

Eventually, they were chatting back and forth like normal, the easy kind of friendship Elaine had missed the past couple days.

It was nice.

If only everything else in her life was so simple and easy.

19

A FEW DAYS LATER AT FRONT BEACHTRO

"I have to admit," Betty said, blowing steam off the top of her coffee, "I hoped you were calling to say you'd changed your mind about joining my dance group."

"I told you not to hold your breath," Elaine chuckled. "It's not going to happen."

It would take a team of wild horses to get her on the dancefloor. John couldn't convince her to go dancing with him even once in the entirety of their marriage. Betty wasn't going to succeed where he had failed.

"I know, I know," Betty sighed. "And it's fine. I'm just as excited to come back and try more on this menu."

"Gregory does a daily special, too," Elaine said. "There's always a reason to come back."

Especially now that Elaine and Annette were on good terms again. Elaine's biggest fear was still that she would lose Charlene or Annette as friends, but in the back of her mind, she'd wondered whether she'd still be welcome at Front Beachtro. Finding a favorite lunch spot was hard work. She didn't want to give this one up.

"Coffees?" Gregory asked as he passed by their table. He never stopped moving, though he did slow to say hi. The dining room was full today, and he'd told Elaine as soon as she'd come through the door that he was down a waitress.

"Remind Annette I love her," he'd sighed melodramatically. "Because the lunch rush might actually be the death of me today."

"Yes, two coffees, please," Elaine said. "And we'll have—" She turned to Betty. "Are you okay with the daily special?"

"Absolutely." Betty closed her menu and passed it to Gregory. "Daily special, please."

"Make that two," said Elaine. "And take your time. We're not in a rush."

Gregory pressed his hands together as if in prayer and bowed. "Bless you both. I'll be as quick as I can."

Betty let out a low whistle. "Poor guy. He looks exhausted."

"But business is good," Elaine said. "It's bittersweet, I suppose."

"For him and for us." Betty looked around and wrinkled her nose. "I'd like to keep coming here for our lunches, but soon enough, reservations may be required."

"I'm sure Gregory will always be able to save a table for us."

Elaine said it, but she wasn't entirely sure she believed it.

Annette had said she didn't want to get in the middle of the fight between Elaine and Charlene, but would she change her mind? At some point, if Charlene insisted on being angry with Elaine, Annette wouldn't have a choice. She couldn't be Switzerland forever.

Even if she could, Elaine didn't want this to last forever.

That was part of the reason she'd asked Betty to lunch.

"So," Elaine started, wanting to cut to the chase but not wanting to look too self-serving, "thanks for coming to lunch."

"Thanks for asking," Betty said. "I was a little afraid another ten years would pass before we met up again. But I'm glad we're both committed to making this a thing. I like talking with you."

Elaine nodded. "Me, too. When we worked together, I always trusted your opinion. And I could trust you to keep secrets."

Betty's eyes narrowed as her mouth tipped up in expectation. "Oh? Do you have a secret, Elaine?"

"No," she said quickly. "Well… no. I have one, but it isn't mine. And that's kind of why I wanted to talk to you."

"Oh, so we're here for a purpose? It's not a lunch date, it's a lunch *meeting*."

Elaine winced. "Yes and no. I wanted to see you, but I also came with a bit of an agenda. Is that okay?"

"Always," Betty insisted. "I'm flattered whether you asked me here to shoot the breeze or for advice. Either way. You know me: I like feeling wanted."

Elaine smiled. "That's great to hear. Because I do want your help."

"Shoot."

Elaine took a deep breath. "Long story short, I broke a friend's trust. I shared private details of her family with another friend of mine, and she is upset about it. I just wonder… what would you do?"

"Can you be any more specific?" Betty asked.

"I'm sorry, I can't. That's what got me into trouble in the first place."

"Okay. Yeah, that makes sense." Betty twisted her mouth to one side and sighed. "When she let you into her private life, did she specifically tell you not to tell anyone else?"

Elaine thought back. "No, not exactly. But she's a very private person. I should have known better."

"Did you apologize?"

"I did," Elaine nodded. "But the person I told is actually a writer. They're here writing a guide back for the Lowcountry, and my friend is worried that her personal life might get published somewhere."

"Oh no. That's not good."

"But I've talked to the writer, and he's said he won't say a word," Elaine said.

"And you trust him?"

Elaine swallowed down a lump of guilt in her throat. "I do. It's why I trusted him with my friend's situation in the first place. I thought he'd be able to help."

Finn was trustworthy. Elaine knew that back when she'd originally told him about Charlene and Margaret, and she knew it now. He hadn't asked to be dragged into this mess—Elaine had made him part of it, and then blamed him for it. She was the one who'd forced his hand on moving out, too.

"Hmm," Betty hummed. "So it doesn't sound like there will be any actual fallout from this situation. Mostly just some emotional damage done, yeah?"

"Yeah, that sounds about right. My friend feels like I betrayed her."

"Do you think you betrayed her?"

"I don't... I don't know," Elaine answered. "Not really. I can see now why she would be worried that I told this writer about her life. If I was in her position, I'd probably be upset, too. But she doesn't know him the way I do."

The question of whether she'd really been naïve had been playing in her head on a loop for days. But the more Elaine thought about it, the more she knew she wasn't. At least not where Finn was concerned.

"I wouldn't have told him if he wasn't trustworthy," she added. "And I didn't tell him in order to gossip about her. I was just trying to help. But I'm not sure that would make for a great apology."

Betty frowned. "No, I'm afraid not."

"What would you do?"

"Well, I would apologize. But I'd leave out all the rationalizations. Especially since you can sympathize with where she is coming from, I say you need to just forget everything else and apologize for sharing anything about her life without asking her permission first."

Elaine nodded. "Okay. I agree. But what if she doesn't forgive me?"

"I hope that won't happen, but there's really no way to know," Betty said. "Unfortunately, that part of it is up to her."

Elaine knew Betty was right, but she wanted there to be something else she could do. Some way to fix it.

When she and John would get in fights, one of them would usually come around in an hour or two and apologize. Most of their fights were about something small and frivolous. The result of a few days of higher than normal tensions that finally bubbled over. Sometimes, the tension would just dissipate. Like a fog burned away by the sun.

But Elaine didn't think her fight with Charlene would vanish quite so easily.

"I'm just not—I don't think I know how to apologize to a friend," Elaine admitted. "That sounds silly, but I never had very many close friends. And none that I ever got in a fight with. I'm just not sure how to say it in a way so she'll forgive me."

Betty gave her a sympathetic smile. "She might not forgive you. Not all at once, anyway."

"What does that mean?"

"It might take several tries," Betty explained. "Friendships are like plants."

Elaine's eyes widened. "Oh no."

"Not much of a green thumb?" Betty laughed.

"My thumb is black. Maybe even charred."

"Friendships are *like* plants. They aren't plants. I think you'll do fine," Betty said. "It just means you need to nurture your friendships."

"Water them, fertilize them, give them light." Elaine was half-teasing, but Betty nodded.

"Exactly! That's exactly it. Like, we didn't see each other for ten years."

Elaine frowned. "Sorry about that."

Betty reached over and grabbed her hand. "Don't apologize. It's my fault, too. We didn't see each other for ten years, so neither of us nurtured our friendship."

"And it fell away," Elaine said quietly.

"It did. But now, we are going to see each other more regularly, right?"

Elaine squeezed Betty's hand back. "Definitely. Very regularly."

Betty smiled. "And our relationship will be stronger for it. If someone had asked me how I knew you a month ago, I would have said you were an old coworker. But now? I'll tell them you're a friend."

Tears burned the backs of Elaine's eyes. She blinked them back. "That makes sense."

"So, when you get in a fight with someone, it's like leaving your full-shade plant in the sun for too long. The leaves get scorched and it dries out. Of course you take it out of the sun and water it, but that doesn't fix everything immediately. You have to nurse it back to health slowly over the course of weeks or months, even."

Elaine nodded. "That makes sense."

"Your friend might not forgive you right away. Maybe not ever," Betty admitted. "But I know you, Elaine. You're a good person with a good heart. My guess? With some tending, she'll come to forgive you and everything will be alright again."

It wasn't the simple fix Elaine had hoped for, but she still felt so much better than she had for days. For the first time since the blow-up, Elaine had hope things could get better.

"Thank you, Betty. That's amazing advice."

Betty shrugged. "Anytime. I have a lot of opinions, so it's nice to be asked to share them for once."

Elaine laughed. "I always want to hear your opinions."

"Don't bite off more than you can chew," Betty teased. "Speaking of, here comes our food."

Gregory hurried out with two steaming plates of shrimp and grits. "Two daily specials. And I have two slices of strawberry shortcake set aside for you in the back. Do you want to wait and have your coffee with your cake?"

"Absolutely. That sounds amazing," Elaine said.

Betty's eyes were fixed on the food in his hands. "You look like an angel to me, Gregory."

Gregory winked at both of them and then whisked away to tend to the burgeoning chaos in the dining room.

The shrimp and grits was so creamy and delicious that they hardly talked while they ate except to compliment the food. And when the strawberry shortcake and coffee came out, Elaine thought she might have actually died and gone to heaven.

"Gregory, where did you get the recipe for that strawberry cake?" Elaine asked when he came to give them the bill. "It was incredible."

"Honestly the best slice of cake I've ever had," Betty said. "And I usually don't even care for cake."

Gregory beamed with pride. "Annette made it."

Elaine's jaw nearly hit the floor. "I knew Annette could bake, but my goodness, she's incredible."

"Tell her that," Gregory said. "I've been trying to talk her into doing some home baking on the side—some wedding cakes or birthday cakes. But she doesn't think she's good enough."

"Well, feel free to tell her two *anonymous* customers raved about her strawberry cake," Elaine said.

"I will," Gregory said. "And you two aren't the only ones. It has made a lot of people very happy today. Unfortunately, if she keeps making it for me, I might need to hire more staff and build an extension on the dining room. We're swamped as it is."

"Oh, right." Elaine jumped up and grabbed her purse. "We'll get out of your hair."

"Oh no," Gregory said. "I didn't mean—"

"We're done, anyway. Aren't we, Betty?"

Betty nodded. "We are. But we'll be back next week." She glanced at Elaine. "Same time?"

Elaine's heart swelled. Betty didn't just talk the talk, she walked the walk.

"Same time," she smiled. "Bring your opinions."

Nurturing a friendship was easier said than done.

Elaine left her lunch with Betty feeling motivated. But by the time she made it home, she realized she didn't exactly have a clear path ahead of her.

She could apologize. But she'd been doing that. Or, trying to, at least.

Charlene wasn't taking her calls. And for good reason. So how was she supposed to apologize? Showing up on her doorstep unannounced felt aggressive and intrusive. Maybe she wasn't great with people, but she knew enough to know that people don't like being surprised like that.

She could write a letter, but there was no way to know if she'd read it. Plus, Elaine wasn't great with words. Not like Finn.

The thought of her old renter struck a guilty chord in her gut. But Elaine ignored it.

Mend one relationship at a time.

Elaine was lying in bed, an unopened book in her lap and a sleepy Ghost curled into her side, when she heard her front door open.

Now that Finn was gone and Annette was so busy with work and spending time with Gregory, the house was quieter. Elaine found the silence even more stifling than it used to be. She'd gotten used to the sounds of someone else moving around her house surprisingly fast.

She knew immediately it was Annette. There was a crash like something had spilled, followed by muffled cursing. That was a dead giveaway.

Elaine smiled to herself.

Annette really was a mess in all the most lovable, endearing ways. Even given everything that had happened in the last couple weeks with her and Charlene, Elaine didn't regret asking Annette to move in. It felt nice to help someone out when they needed it most. If she had the extra space to share, why not?

Suddenly, Elaine went still. She could still hear Annette fumbling around downstairs, but her head was a million miles away.

She had a plan.

20

THE NEXT DAY AT CHARLENE'S HOUSE

Elaine mounted the front steps to Charlene's house on shaky legs.

The closer she'd gotten to Charlene's, the more her nerves had taken driver's seat. Her fingers were trembling around the gift basket she was holding.

"Don't be silly," she muttered to herself. "It's only Charlene."

But this felt an awful lot like an audition.

It had taken everything in her not to barge through Annette's door in the middle of the night and demand her ear. As soon as she heard the sounds of Annette up and moving, she'd slid downstairs and met her in the kitchen.

"I know you don't want to get in the middle, and I don't want to put you in the middle," Elaine had said, "but could you reach out on my behalf? Charlene isn't taking my calls, so could you ask her if she'd be willing to talk with me?"

Annette had agreed and fifteen minutes later come back with an answer. "She'll be home this morning. You can drop by then."

Playing it back now, though, Elaine realized Annette hadn't actually said anything about *asking* Charlene if she wanted to talk to Elaine.

And as soon as Charlene's front door opened to reveal her surprised face, Elaine realized this was a set-up.

So much for Annette not wanting to get in the middle of things.

Elaine held out her basket. "Hi, Charlene."

Charlene eyed it warily, like it might be a trick can of peanuts ready to jump out at her. "What are you doing here, Elaine?"

"I think Annette called you and… set this up." She knew now this was almost certainly not true, but it was easier to explain this way.

"Um… no, she didn't." Charlene narrowed her eyes. "Annette told you to come here?"

Elaine sighed. "Well, yes and no. I asked her to reach out on my behalf. You weren't taking my calls."

"I know." Charlene crossed her arms. She didn't even look angry. She looked… uncomfortable.

Just as uncomfortable as Elaine felt, which only made her feel worse.

"I put together a little basket," Elaine said, offering the basket again. "There are a few bars of white chocolate mixed with nuts and fruit and caramel. My friend Betty recommended the wine. It's a raspberry wine. I've never had it, but it seemed kind of fun. And then there are some fuzzy socks and beeswax lip balm. Just some things I thought—"

"You don't need to get me a gift."

"I know I don't *need* to," Elaine said. "I wanted to."

And Betty had suggested it. Still floundering, Elaine had texted Betty late the night before.

Should I get her a gift? she'd asked.

Maybe a little something with her favorite things in it. Nothing too expensive. You want this to be sweet, not a bribe.

"It's not a bribe," Elaine blurted out. "I mean, I just... I wanted to—I've missed you, Charlene. And I've felt terrible."

Honesty was the best policy. That was what her mom had always said. And if Elaine had learned anything the last week, it was that maybe she should learn to take other people's advice and be leery of her own for a while.

Charlene bit her bottom lip and then finally accepted the basket, albeit reluctantly. "Thanks, Elaine."

"I'm just here to tell you how sorry I am. My intent was never to gossip about you or Margaret," she said. "But obviously, I understand that that is how it came across. And I'm sorry."

"Thank you," Charlene said. "That... that means a lot. Thank you."

For the first time since the idea had popped into her head last night, Elaine's hopes were buoyed. Maybe, just maybe, this was going to work out in her favor.

"I promise not to speak to anyone about your personal life without your express permission. But I also want you to know that I only had the best intentions. I wanted to help."

Charlene pursed her lips. "I know. I know you did. I just... I don't like people knowing about my family's business. About Margaret."

"And I knew that. I should have known better."

"Once people hear something like that, they don't forget it. Do you know what I mean?" Charlene asked. "I love Margaret. Despite everything she has done, I'll always love and forgive her. But other people don't love her like that. This idea they have of her in their heads as a criminal and an addict? That won't ever go away. Which is why I've been so secretive about her... issues."

Elaine's heart cracked. "That makes perfect sense. It's really beautiful, actually. You're doing your best to protect your daughter. I completely understand why you got so upset with me."

"I'm doing my best I can to keep the sky from falling on my head," Charlene laughed bitterly.

"You're doing it well, Charlene. You were right, you know." Elaine twisted her fingers together nervously as she spoke. "When you said I was naïve."

Charlene winced. "No, Elaine. No, I wasn't. I owe you an apology, as well. I shouldn't have—"

"Maybe it was harsh, but it was true," Elaine interrupted. "I don't have many friends. I never have. You are one of the only friends I have that I found on my own. One of the only friends who wasn't a wife of one of John's friends or someone from work. Our relationship is different. It's unique, in a way. And I'm not always sure how to navigate it."

"And you think I know what I'm doing?" Charlene chuckled. "I didn't answer my phone for a week. How's that for mature communication skills?"

Elaine gave her a sad smile. "Well, goodness knows I earned the cold shoulder. If anything, it gave me time to reflect. John was kind of my only friend. My best friend, actually."

"Davy was mine, too," Charlene said quietly. "Maybe you haven't noticed, but I'm not exactly swimming in friends, either."

Elaine frowned. "But don't you do a weekly bridge night with Janie from Front Beachtro?"

"Yeah, but all we do is play a card game. I wouldn't call them friends, per se." Charlene shrugged. "Sometimes, I feel like I only have surface-level people in my life. Not very many people know what's actually going on in my life. Just Annette, Noah... and you."

If this was a children's story, Elaine's heart would have grown two sizes. "Really?"

"Really," Charlene said. "Which is why I think I kind of freaked out. When I found out you told Finn everything, I saw my little family shrinking in front of me, and I lost my temper. I'm sorry about that, Elaine. You deserve better."

Little family. Maybe her heart was growing three sizes.

"Don't apologize. We've already agreed I was in the wrong."

"Perhaps, but I was, too," Charlene said. "I think this is a situation where maybe everybody was a little wrong?"

"That's probably true."

"Maybe that's why we get along so well," Charlene laughed. "Because neither of us are very good at being friends."

Elaine laughed, too. "You know, that would actually make a lot of sense."

Charlene dug through her basket and pulled out the raspberry wine. "How would you like to go crack into this wine that was definitely not a bribe with a fellow misfit?"

"Lead the way. I'd love nothing more."

An Hour Later At Charlene's House

"... I came downstairs after I heard the bang, and Noah was lying at the bottom of the steps with the scooter wrapped around his legs. And Tyler was just standing there in shock."

Elaine gasped. "And Tyler wasn't hurt?"

Charlene shook her head. "There wasn't a scratch on him! Somehow, Noah managed to fall down the stairs and hold Tyler up in the air. I still have no idea how he did it. It was incredible."

"Wonders never cease. Is Noah okay?"

"He's sore," Charlene chuckled. "But fine. And this will teach him to let Tyler ride scooters in the upstairs hallway. I mean, honestly, who thought that was a good idea?"

"Probably Tyler," Elaine said. "I'm sure he loved it."

Charlene sighed. "Oh, he did. He thinks Noah is just about the best person in the world. They get along better than I ever could have hoped."

"That's amazing."

"Yeah, he's handling all of this change so well. Kids are really resilient," she said. "He still misses Annette being here all the time, but he knows we can go see her whenever we want."

"Absolutely. Anytime."

Charlene smiled. "I'm really glad Annette is living with you. I know she can certainly take care of herself, but she hasn't lived on her own in a long time. And now she's pregnant, so… well, I'm just glad you're there with her."

"Oh."

All at once, Elaine remembered why she'd come to Charlene's in the first place. To apologize, yes. Which she'd done.

But also…

"What?" Charlene frowned.

"I just had an idea. Well, I didn't *just* have an idea. I actually had it last night. It's part of why I came over here today." Elaine sighed. "I'm rambling."

"Just a little," Charlene chuckled. "But it's okay. What's up?"

It would have been a good idea to plan a speech. Maybe bring a few notecards. But knocking on the door had been hard enough. She hadn't wanted to overthink it.

"It's still a tender subject, I know. We just hashed everything out, so I don't want to bring it up again, but… I had an idea. A way I could help with Margaret."

Charlene nodded slowly. "Okay…"

"You said Margaret was wanting to stay here after rehab. To use this as a place to get back on her feet. But you didn't love the idea."

"Only because of Tyler," Charlene interjected. "I think it would be hard on him. I just said he was resilient, but—"

"Right. You'd love for her to be here, but with Tyler, things are complicated."

Charlene nodded. "Exactly."

"So, how comfortable would you be with her staying close by?"

"Um, well," Charlene shrugged, "I haven't really thought about it. I didn't think that was an option. Do you know of somewhere?"

"I do. My house."

Charlene blinked at her, and Elaine hurried to explain her thinking.

"I know I shouldn't have told Finn anything about Margaret or your family, but when I did, he told me about his brother's struggles with addiction. He said that he let his brother live with him for a time. His brother relapsed, but Finn said he never regretted giving his brother a safe place to try and get clean. But he said he would have always regretted turning him away." Elaine reached out and grabbed Charlene's hand. "You have a very valid reason for not letting Margaret live with you. Tyler has to be your number one priority. But I have an extra room. Plus, Annette will be there to help, too. I just don't want you to regret saying no. I want you to know that no matter what happens, you tried. *We* tried."

Charlene pulled her hand back, and Elaine thought maybe she'd messed everything up. That maybe she'd crossed another line.

Then she realized Charlene was swiping tears from her eyes.

"Did you practice that speech?" Charlene sniffled.

Elaine shook her head. "No. I probably should have."

"No, it was great," Charlene said. "Straight from the heart."

"It really was. Straight from the heart, that is. Everything I've done, no matter how ill-conceived, really came from the heart." Elaine smiled. "I love you, Char. I want to help."

Without warning, Charlene jumped up and threw her arms around Elaine. "Thank you."

"So is that a yes?" Elaine asked.

"It's a yes from me," Charlene said. "I think it's a great idea. But with Margaret, I never really know what she's thinking. But I'll ask her."

"Okay. I hope she'll say yes. I think we might even be able to find her a job around here. Something part-time. It might help her get back on her feet. John had some friends who might have positions open for—"

Suddenly, Charlene pulled Elaine into another hug. "You're a good friend, Elaine. The island is a better place with you here."

21

THAT AFTERNOON AT ELAINE'S HOUSE

Annette was in the kitchen when Elaine got home, a mountain of baking ingredients piled high on every conceivable surface.

"I'll clean it up," she said immediately. "Don't worry, I'll clean everything up."

Elaine set her purse on the table. "What are you making?"

"I'm not entirely sure yet," she said. "Nothing sounds especially good, but I want to bake."

"You should make strawberry cake, then."

Annette cocked her head to the side. "How did you know about that?"

"I had it at Front Beachtro the other day, and my goodness, Annette: it was so—"

"Wait a minute—Gregory was selling my cake at the restaurant?"

Elaine winced. "At this point, it might be a good idea to just put my foot permanently in my mouth. That's where it prefers to be, anyway."

"He didn't tell me!" Annette said. "I can't believe he did that!"

"Are you mad at him?"

"Well, no," Annette said. "But I'm... shoot, I don't know. If I would have known he was going to sell it, then I would have tried harder to make it look more professional."

"It looked professional to me," Elaine said. "My friend Betty loved it, too. We both raved to Gregory before we even knew it was yours."

Annette frowned, but Elaine couldn't help but notice she looked secretly pleased.

"Still, he should have told me," Annette said. "That's the last time I agree to make him a cake 'just for the heck of it.'"

"Don't do it 'just for the heck of it,'" Elaine said. "Do it because you're talented and people deserve to eat delicious cakes. Because seriously, Annette, it was one of the best cakes I've ever eaten."

Annette arched an eyebrow. "I'm guessing things went well with my sister?"

"What makes you say that?"

Annette waved a hand in Elaine's general direction. "You're peppier than I've seen you in a week. If Charlene had refused to see you, I doubt you'd be in such a good mood."

"Oh yeah," Elaine said. "Which reminds me: so much for you asking her ahead of time. She had no idea I was coming!"

Annette bit back a wince. "Sorry, but she wasn't taking my calls, either. I told you I wasn't taking sides, but I have been encouraging her to talk to you. She got tired of my pestering, I guess. I decided to play matchmaker."

"I'd be annoyed with you if it hadn't worked," Elaine admitted. "We made up and things are okay now. She is going to ask Margaret about staying here with us."

"I'm glad you two made up," she said. "But don't get your hopes up about Margaret. I wouldn't be surprised if she's already changed her mind about living with her mom. Living with a stranger, her aunt, and a newborn may not appeal to her."

Elaine nodded. "I know, but I hope she'll accept. I'll keep the last bedroom upstairs open for her."

"Finn's room?" Annette asked.

"Actually, no. The small room at the end of the hall. It's kind of the catch-all space right now, but I could clear it out for Margaret."

"And you'll rent out the model car room again?"

"Well, actually, I wanted to talk to you about that," Elaine said. "You said Finn told you where he was staying?"

"At the Palm Condos. Number 6A." Annette smirked. "Are you missing him? Planning to visit?"

Elaine hid her blush as she grabbed a plastic storage container out of the fridge. "He's the last stop on the apology tour."

"Sure, sure. Okay." Annette shrugged.

"I'm serious! I blamed him for this whole mess with Charlene, but it wasn't his fault. I owe him an apology."

"Of course," Annette nodded. "And if your apology turns into a dinner and a glass or wine of three, don't worry about getting home late. I won't wait up."

Elaine forced herself not to laugh. Annette didn't need the encouragement.

"If you're not careful, you'll be out of a place to stay, too," she warned with a wink as she headed for the front door.

"Yeah, right," Annette called down the hall. "You love me!"

Elaine couldn't argue with that.

That Afternoon At Palm Condos

The condo was nice, white and tidy with a modern spin. Elaine studied the square silver knocker on the door as she waited to see if Finn was inside.

He was probably out exploring the island. That's what he was there to do, anyway. Not make friends or lounge around waiting for rental owners to show up and apologize for being unreasonable.

She should have called to schedule something. Showing up on his porch was invasive. Stalker-like, even. Finn could call the cops on her, and she wouldn't even be angry. It would be perfectly understandable.

When the door opened, Elaine was so surprised she dropped her plastic storage container.

"Oh no!" Finn bent down to pick it up. "What's this?"

"Leftovers," she blurted. "I, uh… I made too much dinner for myself last night. I thought maybe you'd… like some. But if you don't, I can take it back. I know that's weird. Sorry if—"

Finn pulled the container against his chest protectively. "No, you can't take it back. I want it. Thank you."

"You do?"

Yet again, Elaine had acted without really thinking it through. She'd given Charlene a gift, so it felt wrong to show up to Finn's house emptyhanded. And he did seem to like her cooking.

"I've missed our dinners," he said. "But what brings you here? You seemed a little surprised to see me."

"I thought you might not be here."

"You came to see me when you thought I might not be home?"

"I never claimed it was a good plan."

Finn chuckled. "Well, it's working. Care to come inside? Your cooking isn't the only thing I've missed. I'd love the company."

Elaine was frozen. She'd expected to make some big speech on his front porch. She was prepared to beg for forgiveness.

But Finn was just… inviting her inside. Like nothing whatsoever was amiss.

"I'm going to warm this up. I haven't had lunch yet." He turned his back to her and padded into the house. He was barefoot. He'd always worn slippers at her house. "Come in when you're ready."

Elaine hesitated for only a second before following him inside.

The condo was small. The main room was a square with a sofa and chair in the living room, a bare bones kitchen tucked in the corner, and a two-person dining room table that sat in front of a sliding glass door. There were only two doors at the end of the short hallway. A bedroom and bathroom, Elaine guessed.

Finn pressed a few buttons on the microwave and then turned around, an easy smile on his face.

"It's a little late for lunch, isn't it?" Elaine asked.

He glanced at the clock above the stovetop. "I guess it is. I always lose track of time when I'm writing."

"You've started writing your book?"

"Sort of. I'm trying to organize all of my notes and make sense of the structure. The necessary tedium before the writing."

"Sorry to interrupt," she said. "I won't be long, I just—"

"Don't apologize. I'm glad you're here to distract me."

She gave him a small smile. "Well, I'm glad I'm not bothering you. But I am actually here to apologize. Not for that, but for—for blaming you for something you had nothing to do with."

Strangely, Finn was the one who looked nervous. He shifted on his feet and looked down at the floor.

"I was upset, and I didn't want to be the one at fault," Elaine continued. "It was easier to blame you. So, I'm sorry."

When he looked up, he was smiling. "Apology accepted, of course."

Elaine waited for him to say something else. But he didn't.

"That felt too easy," she said suspiciously.

"Friendships don't have to be hard." He narrowed his eyes. "This does mean we're friends again, right?"

Elaine's face flushed. "Yes. I'm embarrassed I told you we couldn't be. I was so—"

"Upset," he finished. "You were upset, and you made decisions you regret. We've all been there. Believe me."

"Sorry, but it's hard to believe that. You seem so... so put together all the time."

"Well, I got upset when you said we couldn't be friends anymore. So upset I gave up a rented room that was an absolute steal," he said. "I'm not always put together."

"I'm so sorry," she sighed. That phrase was getting an awful lot of mileage in recent days.

"Hey, I wasn't trying to make you feel bad," Finn said. "You're fully forgiven. I'm just saying... we do dumb things when we're hurt. Like, move into a condo that is three times more expensive than anything you budgeted for."

Elaine smiled. Maybe Finn really wasn't trying to make her feel bad, but he was definitely trying to get a message across.

"Are you saying you want to come back to my house?" she asked.

"Oh, what?" Finn asked, feigning surprise. "What gave you that idea?'

Elaine bit back a smile. "Just a thought I had. Because, if you were interested, you're more than welcome to come back. Your room is still—"

"Thank you, I accept," he said quickly.

"Okay then," Elaine said, brows raised.

"Sorry," Finn laughed. "I was hoping to stay in Isle of Palms for a while, but this condo is draining my reserves."

"How long, exactly?"

"I mean, I don't want to speak too soon, but maybe… forever." He shrugged. "A long time, at least. Longer than the month I originally planned."

"Wow. You must have loved that tour of the warship I recommended."

"You know, it was that tour exactly that sold me on staying here forever. Anything to be closer to the USS Yorktown." Finn swooned melodramatically. "But really, I love everything down here. The warmth—from the weather and the people alike—is a big plus. I was never built for cold."

"I hear that. I can't cope when the house drops below seventy. John always said I was like a reptile that way. He joked about getting me a heat lamp once or twice."

"Great idea," Finn said. "I'll go halfsies with you on a heat lamp."

Elaine had missed this casual banter more than she'd let herself realize. It was easy to talk to Finn. In some ways, it reminded her of being with John. She felt effortlessly understood, which wasn't common in her experience.

"Heat lamp or not, you're welcome back at my house as soon as you're ready," Elaine said. "We'd love to have you back."

He grinned. "How's tomorrow?"

"You can get out of the agreement here that quickly?"

"No. I still have another week, but... I'd rather be at your house," he admitted. "I'm tired of eating alone. Plus, Annette promised to teach me how to bake a tres leches cake."

Elaine smiled. "Okay, fine. You can move in tomorrow. But on one condition."

"Which would be?"

"You have to make that cake ASAP. And when you do... save me a slice."

Finn stuck out his hand and they shook on it. "You've got yourself a deal."

22

ONE WEEK LATER AT ELAINE'S HOUSE

"Finley!" Annette called from the kitchen. "You can't leave a pregnant woman alone in the kitchen with fresh whipped cream. Not if you want a decorated cake for dessert."

Finn ducked down, as if he could hide from Annette in the crowd. It wasn't much of a crowd, though. Just a few friends. Well, all of Elaine's friends, really.

Now that everyone was on good terms again, Elaine had decided it was time to launch the next phase of her unofficial plan to become a better friend: throw a party.

"If I ignore her, will she go away?" Finn whispered.

Charlene cackled. "No. Definitely not."

"Sorry, man," Noah agreed. "She's relentless."

"She's scary," Finn corrected. "I've never been through boot camp, but I feel like it would be remarkably similar to baking with Annette. Also, my name is not Finley."

Gregory walked over with a beer and offered it to Finn. "It's worse while she's pregnant. If you stick around long enough, she'll have the baby and calm down. Probably."

"Probably not," Charlene said. "But we can hope."

Finn sighed and headed to the kitchen, earning an encouraging back pat from Charlene on the way.

It was unfortunate that Finn and Charlene didn't meet until after Elaine had dragged Finn into Charlene's personal life and complicated things. But the two of them seemed to be just as forgiving of each other as they were of Elaine. The initial awkward tension between them thawed wonderfully, and now, everyone seemed to be having a good time.

"We need some music in here," Betty said, shimmying her hips to the rhythm in her head. "Mind if I play something?"

Elaine shot a warning look her way. "Only if you don't expect me to dance."

Betty pulled out her phone and connected to the Bluetooth speaker. Something upbeat and poppy Elaine had never heard before started to play.

"I'll get you to dance one day," Betty said. "Charlene has already signed up for a class."

Elaine turned to Charlene with wide eyes. "You're kidding."

"Unfortunately not," Charlene chuckled. "Betty is very persuasive."

Betty grinned. "And I'll get Annette, too. Though she should probably wait until she's had the baby."

"Knowing you, you'll be ringing her up when she's still in the recovery room," Elaine teased.

"It's true. I have no shame." Betty laughed and twirled with the music.

"Can I dance, too?" Tyler darted between his mom and Noah to make it to the center of the room. He jumped and spun around with all the grace a four-year-old could muster.

Everyone clapped to the beat, cheering him on. On his big finish—a move that sent him careening for the corner of the coffee table and forced Noah to dive onto the floor to catch him—Tyler threw both arms in the air and soaked in the applause with a wide grin on his face.

Noah was still lying on the floor in a heap when Tyler wandered back to the hallway to finish his train track.

"Are you okay?" Charlene laughed as she offered him a hand.

"I'm fine," he groaned. "Tyler will either help keep me young or age me prematurely. There's no way to tell yet."

"There's a little way to tell," Elaine said. "But he's worth it, right?"

Noah beamed. "Absolutely."

The doorbell rang, and everyone turned at the sound.

"Who's that?" Betty asked.

"The catering, I think," Elaine said.

Gregory jumped to his feet and hustled to the door. "It's Janie with the food. I'll be right back."

"Catering?" Betty raised her brows. "My, this is a fancy party."

"More like a lazy party. I didn't want to cook for this many people," Elaine laughed. "I asked Gregory if he was interested, and he decided it was a good time to test out Front Beachtro's catering menu."

"Oh yeah," Charlene said. "He mentioned opening the restaurant up for catering a few weeks ago, but I forgot. How exciting."

Gregory came back in with a cardboard box full of aluminum pans. Janie trailed behind with a second box of equipment.

"Give me ten minutes to set up, and I'll be out of your hair," she said as she marched into the kitchen.

Elaine followed to help wherever she could. Though, Gregory and Janie made a great team. They had all the chafing dishes set up in under five minutes.

"You're welcome to stay for dinner, Janie. We have more than enough food."

Janie smiled. "Thanks, Elaine, but I have to get back to the restaurant. Mr. Boss Man put me in charge tonight."

Gregory frowned. "Wait. If you're here, then who's—"

"I left Michael in charge, but don't worry," she said before Gregory could respond, "Joshua is keeping an eye on things from the kitchen. And I was only going to be gone for ten minutes."

"Why not just send Michael out on the delivery, then?" Gregory asked.

"Would you really want him in charge of your dinner?" The horrified expression on Gregory's face was enough of an answer for Janie. "That's what I thought. You're welcome."

Gregory turned to Elaine. "Michael is really nice, but he's new and… clumsy. We're working on it, though."

Elaine snapped her fingers. "Is he the one with the dark hair?"

"And the Harry Potter glasses," Gregory added. "Yeah, that's him."

"I thought so. He waited on me a few days ago. He accidentally refilled my water glass with hot coffee and shattered the glass."

Gregory groaned.

"But he cleaned it up right away," Elaine added. "And he gave me a free dessert to make up for it. I had another slice of Annette's strawberry cake. Overall, I'd say I made out like a thief."

Gregory added something about losing money under his breath as he showed Janie to the door.

A few minutes later, they announced dinner and everyone was happily loading their plates.

"This is quite the spread," Finn said. "I've never had enchiladas and chicken alfredo in the same meal before. But I'm okay with it."

"Sorry. We're trying to see how these recipes hold up to transport," Gregory said. "This is more of a… tasting menu."

"You won't hear a complaint from me." Annette had a pile of pot roast in front of her next to a biscuit covered in sausage gravy. "I requested the biscuits and gravy."

No one at the table voiced any complaints. Mostly because it was hard to talk when you were too busy eating. Strange as it may have been, the food was delicious.

"I'm so glad I decided not to cook," Elaine said when she finished. "This was amazing."

"So good," Charlene agreed.

Finn nodded. "If you're looking for feedback, Gregory, my official review is, 'Yes.'"

Gregory laughed. "Promise to write that in your book?"

"I'll make space for it," Finn promised.

"Right next to your rave review of Elaine's rental?" Charlene teased.

"And the kind words about my baking skills and teaching services." Annette narrowed her eyes threateningly. "Right, Finnley?"

"Of course, Annette." Finn nodded. "And Charlene, if you want me to mention anything about your house flipping business, there's still time. I take bribes in the form of a roof over my head or delicious food. And in the case of Annette, threats."

Everyone laughed. It was music to Elaine's ears. She was so happy that she was close to dancing, though she'd never admit as much to Betty.

After years of mourning the fact that she and John never had children —and then a few more years of mourning John—Elaine finally felt like she had a family of her own.

It was a found family. Not too different from their catered dinner, actually. They didn't all fit together in the classical sense. No one would have arranged for them to be friends. But everyone still had a place at the table.

Even Elaine.

She stood up and cleared her throat. "Well, everyone, thanks for coming to this little impromptu dinner party."

Betty raised her glass and everyone else followed, toasting the food and the company.

"I'm so happy to know all of you and consider you friends." Elaine blinked. She'd barely said anything and she was already on the verge of tears. She swallowed them down. She refused to cry in the middle of her own party. "And that's all I'll say about that. How about we bring out the cake?"

Annette moved to jump up, but Gregory beat her to it. He kissed her head as he spun into the kitchen. "I'll get it, I'll get it."

Gregory was slicing the cake when the doorbell rang again.

Elaine frowned. "Are we missing anyone?"

"Tyler has been playing with our doorbell at home," Charlene said. "Maybe he is—oh, nope. He's under the table."

"Hi!" Tyler yelled from under Noah's chair.

Noah mock-yelled in surprise. "You little rugrat!"

"Gregory, did you order a catered dessert, too?" Annette asked.

Gregory shook his head. "I wouldn't dream of trying to upstage your cake, Netty."

"Oh, it might be one of John's old friends—Mason Dixby. I texted him and his wife Jane on the off chance they were free, but they said they couldn't make it." Elaine shrugged. The doorbell rang again. "But I guess we won't know until I answer it."

Gregory carried the first few plates of cake into the dining room, which immediately pulled everyone's focus from the front door.

Elaine hurried down the hallway so she wouldn't miss her slice of cake. She'd been dreaming about it since she smelled it baking earlier that afternoon.

She was so focused on maybe losing her slice of cake that when she opened the front door, it took her brain a few seconds to process what she was seeing on her front porch.

Or, rather, *who* she was seeing.

The thin young girl with mousy brown hair and wide hazel eyes lifted a hand in greeting. "Hi there."

Elaine blinked. Finally, recognition sunk in. "Margaret?"

23

AT ELAINE'S HOUSE

"Should I have called first?" Margaret asked nervously. "My mom texted me your address, so I thought—I can leave and come back?"

"No! No, come in." Elaine ushered her inside just as a peal of laughter floated down the hallway.

Margaret shrunk back. "Are you having a party? I didn't mean to—"

"No. Well, yes," Elaine said. "But it's just a few friends. Your mom is actually in there."

She couldn't tell if that made Margaret feel better or worse. Her fingers tightened around the handle of her suitcase.

Suitcase. That meant…

"Are you going to stay with me?" Elaine asked quietly.

Margaret's face flushed. "If that's okay? I know it's a lot to ask, but I… I'm desperate. Might as well say it. It's not like it's not already obvious."

Elaine shook her head. "I wouldn't say you're—"

"I would," Margaret said. "This is kind of my last shot to sort myself out."

If Elaine knew anything about Charlene, she'd never give up on Margaret. There would be infinite chances for Margaret to change. But Elaine wasn't going to get involved any more than she already had.

"Well, no matter what, you're welcome here," Elaine said. "The room isn't quite ready yet. It's the last room I have open. It's kind of small, but there's a bed."

"That's all I need. Really. I don't want to intrude."

Elaine draped an arm around Margaret's thin shoulders. "You aren't intruding. I promise. Everyone will be thrilled to see you."

Margaret eyed the sliver of the dining room she could see warily.

"But you don't have to go back there," Elaine said, lowering her voice. "If you want to sneak upstairs for now, I can be discreet. I'm an okay liar when I need to be."

Margaret seemed to consider it, but then she took a deep breath and squared her shoulders. "No, I'm ready. I'm here to make different choices, so that starts now, right?"

"It can if you'd like it to," Elaine smiled.

Margaret smiled back. "But do you think you could get my mom for me? I don't want to surprise her and... and Tyler. I want this to be on her terms."

Elaine hadn't even thought of that. She was touched Margaret had. It seemed like a good sign.

"Of course. I'll be right back."

When she made it back to the dining room, everyone was fixated on Finn's horror stories of baking with Annette that afternoon.

"She actually told me I was opening a can of condensed milk wrong," Finn laughed. "I didn't know that was possible!"

"You were doing it backwards," Annette insisted. "I didn't know *that* was possible!"

Elaine waved to Charlene and brought her into the hallway without anyone noticing.

She'd planned to warn her that Margaret was there before the big reveal, but as soon as Charlene stepped out of the room, she looked to the entryway and froze.

Margaret waved. "Hi, Mom."

A second later, Charlene was at the end of the hall, arms wrapped around her daughter. The two whispered to each other. Charlene's shoulders shook with quiet sobs.

Tears pricked the backs of Elaine's eyes. She looked away, trying to give the two some privacy.

"You're going to stay here?" Charlene asked when the two finally disentangled.

"Yeah. I want to get myself sorted out. I'm... I'm sorry about—"

"Later," Charlene said gently. "We can talk about everything later. I'm just glad you're here."

"Me, too," Margaret said. "I didn't have anywhere else to go. I'm only here thanks to Elaine."

Charlene turned around and looped Elaine into a hug. "Yeah, thanks to Elaine."

Elaine had promised herself she wouldn't insert herself into anyone else's family drama anymore. But in this case, she made an exception.

She hugged Charlene and Margaret in the entryway, just as Ghost ran up out of nowhere and wound himself like a scarf around her legs.

In the dining room, under the picture of John where Elaine used to eat alone, the rest of her friends were rolling with laughter. Every room was occupied, happy noise filled the house, and a once-lonely cat's contented purr underscored everything.

What could be better?

Turn the page to check out a sneak preview of my bestselling women's fiction novel, NO HOME LIKE NANTUCKET!

SNEAK PREVIEW OF NO HOME LIKE NANTUCKET

If you loved **The Beach Baby**, *you'll fall head over heels for the Benson family in my beloved Sweet Island Inn series, set on the gorgeous island of Nantucket.*

Take a sneak preview below of Book 1 in the series, NO HOME LIKE NANTUCKET.

∽

**NO HOME LIKE NANTUCKET:
A Sweet Island Inn Novel (Book 1)**

Nantucket was their paradise—until reality came barging in.

An unexpected pregnancy.

A marriage on the rocks.

A forbidden workplace romance.

And a tragedy no one could have seen coming.

Take a trip to Nantucket's Sweet Island Inn and follow along as Mae Benson and her children—the Wall Street queen Eliza, stay-at-home mom Holly, headstrong chef Sara, and happy-go-lucky fisherman Brent—face the hardest summer of their lives.

Love, loss, heartbreak, hope—it's all here and more. Can the Benson family find a way to forgive themselves and each other? Or will their grief be too much to overcome?

Find out in **NO HOME LIKE NANTUCKET.**

Click here to start reading now!

❧

Chapter One: Mae

Mae Benson never ever slept in.

For each of the one thousand, two hundred, and eleven days that she'd lived at 114 Howard Street, Nantucket, Massachusetts, she'd gotten up with the dawn and started her morning the second her eyes opened. It wasn't because she was a busybody, or compulsive, or obsessive. On the contrary, snoozing for a while was tempting. Her bed was soft this morning. The first fingers of springtime sunlight had barely begun to peek in through the gauzy curtains that hung over the window. And she was in that perfect sleeping position—warm but not too warm, wrapped up but not too tightly.

But force of habit could sometimes be awfully hard to break. So, being careful to make as little noise as possible, she slid out from underneath the comforter, tucked her feet into the fuzzy slippers she'd received for her sixtieth birthday last year, and rose.

Her husband, Henry, always called her his little hummingbird. He'd even bought her a beautiful handblown hummingbird ornament for Christmas last year from a glassblower down by the wharf. It had jade-green wings, little amethysts for eyes, and a patch of ruby red on its chest. She loved how it caught and refracted the winter sunbeams, and she always made sure to put it on a limb of the tree where it could see the snow falling outdoors.

"Flitting around the house, are we?" Henry would say, laughing, every time he came downstairs from their master bedroom to find Mae buzzing from corner to corner. She would just laugh and shake her head. He could make fun of her all he wanted, but the fact remained that each of the little projects she had running at all times around the house required love and care from the moment the day began.

She ran through the list in her head as she moved silently around the bedroom getting dressed for the day. She needed to water the plants on the living room windowsill, the ones that her daughter, Sara, had sent from her culinary trip to Africa and made her mother promise to keep alive until she could retrieve them on her next visit. Crane flowers, with their gorgeous mix of orange- and blue-bladed leaves; desert roses, with their soft blush of red fading into the purest white; and her favorites, the fire lilies, that looked just like a flickering flame.

She had to check on the batch of marshmallow fluff fudge—a Mae Benson specialty—that she'd left to set in the freezer overnight. Her friend Lola, who lived down the street, had just twisted her ankle badly a few days prior and was laid up at home with a boot on her leg. Mae didn't know much about ankle injuries, but she had a lot of hands-on experience with fudge, so she figured she'd offer what she knew best.

She should also start coffee for Henry—lots of cream and sugar, as always. Henry had an outing planned that morning with Brent to go check on some fishing spots they'd been scheming over for the last few weeks. Mae knew he was excited about the trip. He'd been exhibiting trademark Happy Henry behavior all week long—eyes lighting up with that mischievous twinkle, hands rubbing together like an evil mastermind, and the way that he licked the corner of his lips, like he could already taste the salt air that hung on the wind and feel the bouncing of the boat as it raced through the waves.

Just before she turned to leave the bedroom and start her day, she looked over at her husband. He was sleeping on his side of the bed, snoring softly like he always did. It was never enough to wake her, thankfully. Not like Lola's ex-husband, who'd been a snorer of epic proportions. Henry hadn't bothered a single soul in the six and a half decades he'd been alive on this earth. Matter of fact, she couldn't think of a single person who disliked him—other than Mae herself, whenever he took the liberty of dipping into the brownie batter, or when he insisted on sneaking up behind her while she was cooking, nipping at the lobe of her ear, then dancing away and laughing when she tried to swat him with a spoon and inevitably sprayed chocolate batter all over the kitchen.

But the truth of the matter was that she could never bring herself to stay irked at him. It wasn't just his physical looks, although he certainly wasn't hurting in that department. The same things she'd fallen in love with at that Boston bar forty-plus years ago were still present and accounted for. The long, proud nose. Full lips, always eager to twitch into a smile. Bright blue eyes that danced in the sunlight when he laughed, cried, and—well, all the time, really. And that darn shock of hair that was perpetually threatening to fall over his forehead. She reached over and smoothed it out of his face now. Time had turned his sun-drenched blondness into something more silvery, but in Mae's eyes, he was all the more handsome for it.

But, even more than his good looks, Mae loved Henry's soul. He was a selfless giver, an instant friend to every child who'd ever come across his path. He loved nothing more than to kneel in front of an awestruck five-year-old and present him or her with some little hand-carved trinket, one of the many he kept in his pockets to whittle whenever he had an idle moment. She loved that he laughed and cried in all the wrong places during romantic comedies and that he knew how to cook—how to *really* cook, the kind of cooking you do with a jazz record crooning through the speakers and a soft breeze drifting in through an open window.

She let her hand linger on Henry's forehead just a beat too long. He didn't open his eyes, but his hand snaked up from underneath the sheets and threaded through Mae's fingers.

"You're getting up?"

"Can't waste the day away."

It was a ritual, one they'd been through practically every morning for as long as either could remember. For all that he'd become a proud father to four children, a state-record-holding fisherman, a much-sought-after contractor and builder on the island of Nantucket, Henry loved nothing so much as to stay in bed for hours, alternating between sleeping and poking Mae until she rolled over and gave him the soft kisses he called her "hummingbird pecks." There was a perpetual little boy spirit in him, a playfulness that another six or sixty decades couldn't extinguish if it tried.

"Stay with me," he murmured. "The day can wait a few more minutes, can't it?" His eyes were open now, heavy with sleep, but still gazing at her fondly.

Mae tapped him playfully on the tip of the nose. "If it was up to you, 'a few more minutes' would turn into hours before we knew it, and then I'd be scrambling around like a chicken with my head cut off, trying to get everything done before Holly, Pete, and the kids get here tonight."

Holly was Mae and Henry's middle daughter. She and her husband, Pete, were bringing their two kids to Nantucket to spend the weekend. Mae had had the date circled on her calendar for months, excited at the prospect of spoiling her grandkids rotten. She already had oodles of activities planned—walks downtown to get rock candy from the corner store, sandcastles at the beach, bike rides down to 'Sconset to ogle the grand houses the rich folks had built out on that end of the island.

Grady was a little wrecking ball of a seven-year-old boy, and Mae knew that he'd love nothing so much as building a massive sandcastle and then terrorizing it like a blond Godzilla. Alice, on the other hand, was still as sweet and loving as a five-year-old girl could be. She let Grandma Mae braid her long, soft hair into fishtails every morning whenever they were visiting the island. It was another ritual that Mae treasured beyond anything else. Her life was full of those kinds of moments.

"It ain't so bad, lying in bed with me, is it?" Henry teased. "But maybe I just won't give ya a choice!"

He leaped up and threw his arms around Mae's waist, tugging her over him and then dragging them both beneath the covers. Mae yelped in surprise and smacked him on the chest, but Henry was a big man—nearly six and a half feet tall—and the years he'd spent hauling in fish during his weekend trips with Brent had kept him muscular and toned. When her palm landed on his shoulder, it just made a thwacking noise, and did about as much good as if she'd slapped a brick wall. So she just laughed and let Henry pull her into his arms, roll over on top of her, and throw the comforter over their heads.

It was soft and warm and white underneath. The April sun filtered through the bedsheets and cast everything in a beautiful, hazy glow. "You've never looked so beautiful," Henry said, his face suspended above hers.

"Henry Benson, I do believe you are yanking my chain," she admonished.

"Never," he said, and he said it with such utter seriousness that Mae's retort fell from her lips. Instead of poking him in the chest like she always did whenever he teased her, she let her hand stroke the line of his jaw.

He pressed a gentle kiss to her lips. "Stay with me for just a few more minutes, Mrs. Benson," he said. She could feel him smiling as he kissed her. She could also feel the butterflies fluttering in her stomach. Forty-one years of marriage and four children later, and she still got butterflies when her husband kissed her. Wasn't that something?

"All right, Mr. Benson," she said, letting her head fall back on the pillows. "Just a few more minutes."

Henry grinned and fell in next to her, pulling her into his embrace. She could feel his heartbeat thumping in his chest. Familiar. Dependent. Reliable. Hers. "You just made my day."

"But I'm warning you," she continued, raising one finger into the air and biting back the smile that wanted to steal over her lips. "If you start snoring again, I'm smothering you with a pillow."

"Warning received," Henry said. "Now quit making a fuss and snooze with me for a while, darling."

So Mae did exactly that. Sara's plants could wait.

Click here to keep reading!

JOIN MY MAILING LIST!

Click the link below to join my mailing list and receive updates, freebies, release announcements, and more!

JOIN HERE:

https://sendfox.com/lp/19y8p3

ALSO BY GRACE PALMER

Sunny Isle of Palms

The Beach Baby

The Beach Date

The Beach B&B

The Wayfarer Inn

The Vineyard Sisters

The Vineyard Mothers

The Vineyard Daughters

Sweet Island Inn

No Home Like Nantucket (Book 1)

No Beach Like Nantucket (Book 2)

No Wedding Like Nantucket (Book 3)

No Love Like Nantucket (Book 4)

No Secret Like Nantucket (Book 5)

No Forever Like Nantucket (Book 6)

Willow Beach Inn

Just South of Paradise (Book 1)

Just South of Perfect (Book 2)

Just South of Sunrise (Book 3)

Just South of Christmas (Book 4)